ANNIE AND THE RIPPER

by Tim Champlin

FIRST SOFTCOVER EDITION

ISBN-13: 978-1-61706-037-3

Cover art by Greg Smallwood
Cover design by Alva J. Roberts
Published by Pill Hill Press
First Printing: August 2010

Visit us online at www.pillhillpress.com

FOR LIZ AND PATRICK,
WHO LIKE THIS SORT OF THING

Also by Tim Champlin

Summer of the Sioux
Dakota Gold
Staghorn
Shadow Catcher
Great Timber Race
Iron Trail
Colt Lightning
King of the Highbinders
Flying Eagle
The Last Campaign
The Survivor
Swift Thunder
Deadly Season
Wayfaring Strangers
Lincoln's Ransom
The Tombstone Conspiracy
A Trail to Wounded Knee
Treasure of the Templars
By Flare of Northern Lights
White Lights Roar
Raiders of the Western & Atlantic
Fire Bell in the Night
The Blaze of Noon
Devil's Domain—Far From the Eye of God
Territorial Rough Rider
Cold Cache
West of Washoe
Beecher Island
Tom Sawyer and the Ghosts of Summer

ANNIE AND THE RIPPER

by Tim Champlin

Pill Hill Press
Chadron, Nebraska

AUTHOR'S NOTE

Everyone loves a mystery. Jack the Ripper is still a mystery. His legend, ever new, continues to evolve. What makes the case of this notorious serial killer so fascinating is the fact that no one was ever arrested or tried for the murders. He remains unknown to this day. For a century and a quarter, latter-day sleuths—Ripperologists—have attempted to positively identify the slasher of prostitutes who terrorized London's East End during the last few months of 1888. Over the years, many authors have put forth their arguments for this suspect or that suspect, some of them hardly known in 1888, as being the Ripper. But there's always at least one hole in every carefully crafted theory that lets the air out of the balloon. The case has never been solved. Now, several generations after the murders, it's not likely to be, barring some startling factual evidence that has yet to come to light.

Also in the late 1880s, Annie Oakley was the internationally acclaimed star of William F. Cody's Wild West Show, which performed in London for six months in 1887, the jubilee year of Queen Victoria's coronation. The show also returned to perform in London and Europe in 1889.

What if Annie Oakley and Jack the Ripper had met? I was intrigued by the possibilities. What would have happened if this demented serial killer of women had come up against the courageous, athletic woman who was very likely the world's most skillful rifle and pistol shot?

What if...?

I had to know. So, I created this novel to find out.

The pairing of these two disparate historical characters is not as implausible as it may first appear. Annie's own factual background as an abused child slave would have given her a strong motivation for cooperating with the law to assist in luring and trapping the Ripper.

I wove many of the known facts of the Ripper case into the story, but created my own version of Inspector Abberline of Scotland Yard, who was prominent in investigating the murders. My story is historical fiction, a blend of what did happen and what could have happened.

So, settle in and immerse yourself in this Victorian tale where fact and legend envelope you thicker than a London fog.

PROLOGUE

3:10 a.m.
August 31, 1888
London, England

"Polly, come along with me. You can share my room."

Two women stood on the sidewalk in front of a darkened lodging house.

"I'll not be beholden to you, Sarah." Polly made as if to turn away.

"It's all right," the first woman pled, "you can save your money."

"I've earned my doss money twice tonight, but I drank it up." She giggled. "I can earn it again, don't you fret."

"I know you can. It's just that the night's nearly gone. Come, get some rest. Sleep it off and we'll start fresh tomorrow evening," Sarah said.

"Not a bit of it. There's plenty of fish out there yet, and I'll snag one." She disengaged herself from Sarah's arm. "I've got on a jolly bonnet that'll fetch 'em." She leaned forward as if to show off her hat, and nearly lost her balance. She straightened up, moving carefully. "I'll be back shortly." She reeled off down the street. "Don't wait up," she said gaily over her shoulder.

Twenty minutes later Polly was more than a half-mile away, moving along deserted Bucks Row, clinging to the arm of a man in dark clothing a few inches taller than she. They paused by a head-high wooden fence that enclosed an empty stable yard between two buildings.

"This all right?" the man asked in a low voice.

"Why, sure, luv," she said. "Good as any."

He pushed open the gate and followed her inside the enclosure.

With practiced ease, she flipped up her skirts over her backside and leaned forward, palms flat against the fence.

The man moved in behind her and fumbled with his pants. Then, swift as a lunging panther, his hands shot forward and locked around her slender neck. She sprang upright, gurgling, clawing at his powerful grip. The silent, deadly struggle continued for long seconds, stretching out to a minute…then two. She went limp and he lowered her to the ground, face first. A long knife appeared in his hand. Yanking her head back by the hair, he reached around from behind and, with two swift sweeps of the blade, slashed her throat, deeply and thoroughly.

He paused, panting, and looked over the fence. The street remained deserted. He rolled her over onto her back, threw up her dress and made four frenzied hacks at her abdomen, swearing when the knife caught in her voluminous clothing and waistband. An expletive exploded from his lips as he stabbed at her groin area. Finally sated, he stood up, breathing heavily, and wiped the blade on her skirt. He slipped the knife back into a leather sheath sewn inside his coat. Gliding out, he left the gate open and cat-footed away, blending with the shadows.

CHAPTER 1

August, 31, 1888

Bong!...Bong!...Bong!...Bong!
Measured strokes from the clock tower in Spitalfields tolled four—a deep-black, vulnerable hour of the London night. The last echoing chime faded into silence, and the quiet breath of slumber settled once again over the sprawling city. In Bucks Row, a workingmen's street in the East End, a corner gaslight hissed softly, forming a cottony halo of light in the summer fog.

The distant, rhythmic clicking of a trotting horse broke the silence. Its staccato clatter of iron shoes on cobblestones grew louder and a Hansom cab passed the streetlight. Fifty yards beyond, the horse and cab drew to a stop where lantern beams were stabbing the darkness.

Two men alighted. Scotland Yard Inspector, Frederick George Abberline, rubbed his tired eyes and bit his lip to keep from snapping at the uniformed patrolman who had roused him from a sound sleep in his bachelor's quarters. No need to upbraid a man for doing his duty. Odd hours were part of the job; criminals didn't fancy daylight.

Abberline sniffed the familiar odors of rotting cabbage, limed outhouses, and cigar smoke as he followed the constable toward a knot of men clustered near a five-foot wooden fence enclosing a stable yard.

"Make way!"

Curious men in work clothes fell back for the uniformed patrolman and Abberline to reach the inner circle.

"Hold your light down a bit," a kneeling man directed, bending low over a pile of rumpled clothing. Two constables redirected the beams from their bullseye lanterns and Abberline, looking over the kneeling man's shoulder, saw the glint of wet blood. Recognizing the back of the hatless gray head of his friend, Doctor Andrew Llewellyn, the chief inspector stood patiently for another minute or two to allow the doctor time to finish a cursory examination.

Frederick Abberline wondered why he'd been called. As a detective of long-standing and considerable repute, he was accustomed to being brought in solely to assist with unusually difficult murder cases. In London's Whitechapel district, where he was known and respected, murders were only slightly less frequent than deaths from malnutrition, alcohol, and various untreated diseases. The constable who had come for him mentioned something about this being a particularly gruesome crime.

Finally, the middle-aged doctor struggled up from the paving stones, and turned around. "Ah, inspector. You made good time. The handcart ambulance is on the way. If it's all right with you, we'll take the body to Old Montague Street Workhouse infirmary mortuary. I'll need more time and light to do a thorough examination…"

He paused as Abberline turned to one of the constables. "Let me borrow that." He reached for the man's bullseye lantern, pointed the beam down and squatted next to the body. His sensitive nose picked up the smells of blood, urine and feces.

"Disemboweled," the doctor said quietly to Abberline, "and throat slashed from side to side so deep it nearly severed her head."

The woman's eyes were still open, as if looking in vain for her attacker—a disconcerting sight. The gaping wound in her throat was spattered with congealed blood. Abberline gingerly lifted her skirts and noted rolls of shiny intestines and internal organs bulging from the vast cut across her abdomen. Her hands were open at

4

her sides, the left just touching the stable yard gate. He dropped the layers of petticoats over the gruesome sight, clamping his jaw angrily at the brutality of the attack. Then he drew his notepad and pencil and quickly sketched the position and attitude of the body.

"Anyone see anything?" He directed his question to the small group at his back without looking up.

There was a murmur of negative answers.

"I found 'er, sir," a voice said.

Abberline turned his head. "What time?"

"About half three, I'd say."

Doctor Llewellyn nodded. "Upper arms and thighs still warm. She's been dead not more than thirty minutes."

"What's your name?" Abberline asked, pencil poised.

"Charles Cross, sir. I was walking to m'job as a car-man in Broad Street when I saw what looked like a tarp someone had dropped over here by the gate to the stable yard. Took a closer look and saw 'twas a woman laid out with her petticoats hiked up. Thought at first she was dead drunk and passed out, so I called out to Robert Paul who was passing by on his way to work. Her hands were cold, but Robert thought he could feel her heart beatin' and her chest movin' with breath. We didn't have a light or nothin', but just then a constable come by on his rounds with a lantern and we see she'd been gashed sumthin' 'orrible. She was dead for sure by then."

"That's a fact, inspector. I'm Constable John Neil. I signaled with my lantern for John Thain, the constable from Brady Street and he went to fetch Doctor Llewellyn down Whitechapel Road. While we waited, I rang the bell at Essex Wharf across the road from the stable here and asked if anyone had heard a disturbance. The manager, Mr. Purkiss, said he and his wife were asleep and heard nothing. Sergeant Kerby arrived about the time the doctor did and he inquired at the next house here where Emma Green and her daughter live. Same story. Nobody heard a thing."

"Constable Neil, take down everyone's statement while things are fresh in mind," Abberline directed. "You know the procedure. Question more of the neighbors. Record all the information you can.

Don't neglect the smallest detail."

"Yessir."

The ambulance arrived just then and the two constables lifted the woman onto the canvas stretcher, smearing their hands with blood. Abberline noted the reason he'd seen little blood on the sidewalk and in the gutter—most of it had run underneath the woman and been absorbed by her clothing.

To prevent the wheeled stretcher from bouncing on the rough street, Abberline instructed the two workhouse inmates who'd been sent to pick up the body to lift the handcart clear of the pavement. They complied, trundling the covered corpse off toward the temporary morgue, several blocks away.

The two men who discovered the body began dictating their stories to the constables. The half-dozen workmen who were on their way home or to the early shift dispersed, walking in the middle of the street and casting glances into the black shadows.

"We can take my Hansom that's waiting," Abberline said to the doctor. The two men climbed in and pulled the half door closed over their legs.

"The workhouse in Montague Street," Abberline called up to the driver, who snapped the reins and the horse clopped off at a walk.

"Cigar?" Dr. Llewellyn offered.

"Don't mind if I do," Abberline answered, taking the slim smoke.

The doctor selected one for himself from the flat cigar case and struck a light for both of them. Abberline noticed how tired and lined his friend's face appeared in the flare of the sulfur match.

"I thought you gave up smoking," Abberline remarked after a couple of puffs.

"I tried. But I find I need one of these to get the smell out of my nostrils after something like that."

"What do you make of it?" Abberline asked.

"My job is to examine, record and report," the doctor replied. "Yours is to analyze, speculate and deduce. Mine is the 'what'; yours

6

is the 'why'. I'd rather have my job any day than yours."

Abberline gave a harsh cough. "You're absolutely correct. That was a ghastly murder. Now I must figure out a motive. A poor prostitute, who wasn't particularly young or pretty, in a poor section of town. I suppose we'll find out who she is. Did she have anything in her pockets, or carry a handbag?"

"Didn't look. If there was anything on the ground, the constables will find it. I'm sure she had friends in the area. Word will get around quickly and someone will come in to identify her."

"We can assume she had little or no money. Likely only trying to earn enough for a bed or a gin. Robbery wasn't the motive."

"Even if she had a pocketful of gold coin, there was no justification for the mutilation," the doctor said.

"The work of a madman, indeed."

The end of the doctor's cigar glowed red in the dim light. "There's no shortage of those in London. The asylums are full."

"A man who hated women, or prostitutes for some reason," Abberline muttered, thinking aloud.

"Possibly. Or a man who was angered about something entirely unrelated, and just took it out on this poor woman."

"A man who'd contracted syphilis from a prostitute might be vengeful, or the disease could have caused a mental derangement…" His voice trailed off.

"There's no real cure for that," Dr. Llewellyn said. "It can be latent in the blood for years while attacking the brain cells. Madness can come on gradually."

Abberline sighed. "We could speculate 'til doomsday, and be no closer to the answer."

"Unfortunately, medical science knows very little about the brain and its functions."

"All logic is thrown out when dealing with a madman."

"Some of them do follow a pattern of behavior," the doctor said. "At least I've seen the same bizarre actions being performed over and over by certain hospitalized mental patients."

"Yes, whoever did this might repeat his performance in the

near future if he's that sort of violent lunatic. If this man isn't caught right away, I'll discuss with my superiors some cautionary measures that might forestall future attacks. It'll involve more foot patrolmen in the district, a lot of door-to-door legwork and interviews, checking all the known felons, and released mental patients in Whitechapel."

"Why only Whitechapel?"

"I suspect the killer didn't travel far to commit this crime, that he lives in the area and is not someone who would arouse any suspicion among the shopkeepers, landlords or street women. It was done quietly, since no one nearby heard any kind of commotion or cry."

"No woman cries out after her throat is slashed."

"Wouldn't there be a spurt of blood if the killer gashed the carotid? He'd be covered in it."

"Not if the attack came from behind, which I'd guess it did. Probably have some staining of the hands and arms, though, even if he wore gloves."

"From all accounts, that man, Cross, came within a few minutes of encountering the killer."

"Since my surgery is just down the street, I know of quite a number of rather odd people in this neighborhood, alcoholics, eccentrics with very strange obsessions, several teetering on the edge of sanity, barely able to function in their hand-to-mouth existence, men and women from sordid backgrounds to whom violence is a way of life." Dr. Llewellyn flicked the ash off his cigar and looked across at Abberline. "You think this is his first crime?"

Abberline thought for a moment. "Possibly not. I recall at least two similar unsolved murders just recently. Last April a prostitute, who usually went by the name of Emma Smith, was attacked about this time of the morning. She was only bruised up, but died next day. Death was the result of an infection brought on by the brutal insertion of some object into the vagina that ruptured a membrane. Then there was another murder earlier this month. A Martha Turner, or Tabram, was found on the landing of the stairs up to a lodging house. She'd been stabbed thirty-nine times."

"Possibly the same killer?"

"Hard to say. If so, he's becoming progressively brutal."

The doctor nodded. "The man was either very insane or very enraged if he eviscerated a corpse."

The Hansom cab stopped in front of the workhouse, Abberline paid the driver, and the two men waited in the side yard for the arrival of the inmates with the body on the stretcher. When it arrived fifteen minutes later, Dr. Llewellyn sent one of the men to fetch the director to unlock the mortuary and allow them to place the corpse on the examining table inside. The doctor turned up the gas jets to their brightest, stripped off his waistcoat and rolled up his sleeves.

"If you don't mind, I'll pop across the street to the Boar's Head for a bite of breakfast," Abberline said, having seen enough gore for the moment. "I'll wait for you out here in the courtyard when I get back."

"I'll be at least an hour," Doctor Llewellyn said.

Abberline nodded and turned away, scrubbing a hand over his face. His bushy sideburns obscured the fact that the rest of his face was covered with stubble. With autumn coming, maybe he should grow a full beard and not have to shave at all. But a beard was nearly suffocating to him, and made him look older than his forty-six years. He was sliding into middle age as a bachelor. At this time of night, in the darkest hour before dawn, his whole being was at its lowest ebb, and he almost wished he had a wife to go home to. Well, he'd chosen this way of life, and he'd stick with it. The only thing preventing him from becoming stodgy and set in his middle years was the complete unpredictability of his job that kept his mind sharp and his body active. No wife would take kindly to a husband who had to jump out of bed in the middle of the night and go running off to a dangerous part of the city to look at the bloody corpse of a woman.

He glanced up and down the deserted street, seeing the wet paving stones shining under street lamps that barely penetrated the fog at each end of the block. Taking a deep breath of the cool air, he crossed the street, his rubber heels making little noise in the stillness. A cup of tea with biscuit and jam would set him right. He smiled grimly as he pulled open the door of the all night public house.

"Find anything new?" Abberline asked the doctor ninety minutes later as they stood in the empty courtyard next to the workhouse.

"Not much. Two women who're lodging next door showed up and identified her as Mary Ann Nichols. Went by the name of Polly. She was in her forties. She's borne children. The women said she'd shown up drunk earlier at the lodging house, but didn't have the price of a bed so she was turned away. 'I'll soon get my doss money,' the women quoted her as saying. 'See what a jolly bonnet I've got now? That'll fetch 'em.' One of the women tried to get her to come and share a room with her, but Polly refused and staggered off. She was found less than three-quarters of a mile from where she was last seen."

The doctor paused. Abberline felt his throat tighten. The mutilated body was taking on the personality of one Polly Nichols, a pitiful human being. Abberline thought he should be over such emotional reaction to every victim whose murder he investigated. But, then, if he distanced himself from all feeling, he might as well go home and work crossword puzzles.

"I'm sure others will come forward and give us more details of her life, once her death becomes known," the doctor was saying. "I found damage to the laryngeal structures, and petechiae was present in her face and around the eyes…"

"What's that?" Abberline interrupted.

"Showers of tiny pin-point hemorrhages under the skin consistent with strangulation. She'd been choked, probably to unconsciousness, before her throat was slashed, so she very likely never knew what happened."

In the graying dawn, the two men looked at each other and Abberline knew this last statement was meant to blunt his own horror of imagining what Polly Nichols must have suffered in her last moments.

"You want the details?"

He shook his head. "You summarized it well enough for now. There'll be a coroner's inquest in a few days. Unless we catch the killer first, the jury will conclude with those familiar words, '… death caused by person or persons unknown.'" He sighed. "I'll read your full report later. Right now, I'll be getting home. Have to be at the office in about two hours."

"Good day to you, then," Doctor Llewellyn said, shaking his hand.

"Thanks for your help."

Abberline saw so sign of a cab at this early hour, so he decided to walk the mile to his lodging house.

The sun was peeking over the roofline and dissipating the night mist. Its rays caught the colors of a garish poster plastered to a brick wall. Although it'd been there all summer and he'd passed it many times, he'd never bothered to look at it. The heavy paper was torn in places and showing the effects of rain and sun, but the huge lettering and bigger than life images were still strong. He paused and read: "BUFFALO BILL'S WILD WEST, And Congress of Rough Riders of the World".

"Huh!" he snorted as his eyes glanced down over the rest. The poster was covered with scenes of Indians on horseback, wearing war bonnets and pursuing a stagecoach, covered wagons, mounted cowboys. In a circular frame was the now-familiar picture of Buffalo Bill Cody, big hat, goatee and all. Below Cody's face was the image of a long-haired girl in a wide-brimmed hat, medals pinned to her jacket, and the words, "Annie Oakley—The Peerless Wing and Rifle Shot". In the background were smaller images of her firing a rifle and a pistol at various thrown and held targets.

He yawned and moved on. Show business. These Americans had come to England to make money from thousands of his gullible countrymen. A bunch of whooping Indians and cowboys, riding around shooting blanks at each other and at buffalo. It was all a sham, like card tricks. Annie Oakley's fancy shooting was undoubtedly

11

fake—designed to fool the eye. Nobody, especially a young woman in a man's sport, could be as good as she was reported to be. He had to admit she was good looking. But at that show, a spectator would never get close enough to really see her. He wondered how good he would be if pitted against her. He hadn't been on the practice range for months. His weapon was for self-defense only. And, although confident he was in no danger on the streets of Whitechapel, he was nonetheless reassured by the lump under his coat, a shoulder holster containing his Adams revolver.

CHAPTER 2

2:20 p.m.
August 31, 1888
Earl's Court, London

The canvas door of the white tent was flung back and Annie Oakley strode out, cheeks flushed and full lips compressed.

"Uh, oh! Mad as a wet hen," Matt Vickers muttered, sliding behind the corner of a nearby wagon and avoiding eye contact with those orbs she flashed around, apparently probing for a target. Being her "gun boy" and messenger didn't mean being the brunt of her fury.

But she didn't notice him. Smoothing her pleated riding skirt, she moved gracefully toward the entrance to the arena, the pearl studs on her hand-sewn leggings catching the light. Matt saw her shrug and flex her arms and shoulders under the doeskin jacket to be sure she was loose and ready as she poised like an athlete ready to spring.

"Now, ladies and gentlemen, I have the distinct honor of bringing you the world's greatest sharpshooter..." Harvey Archibald's voice boomed hollowly through the megaphone outside in the Earl's Court Exhibition Grounds. "...I give you the incomparable, *Annie Oakley!*"

A roustabout pulled the canvas drape aside. Annie bounded into the arena and turned an acrobatic handspring over the gun table,

13

snatching up a 16-gauge shotgun as she went. The drape fell back into place, blotting the sight, but Matt pictured her swinging the gun to her shoulder. *Bang! Bang! Bang!* He knew from the wave of applause that her wing shots had blasted 3 colored glass balls out of the air, tossed by her manager/husband, Frank Butler.

Matt had seen her twenty-minute performance dozens of times, but he never tired of viewing her smooth display of skill.

The big boss, Colonel William F. Cody, in an astute move to capture the audience early, had positioned her act at the top of the show, right after the grand parade, which opened every performance.

"What's wrong with her?"

Matt turned to see his 19-year old Sioux friend, Crowfoot, standing a few feet away, observing.

"Nothing gets by you, does it, Crofe?" Matt said. "She's mad as hell."

"What for?" the Indian inquired, gliding forward and pulling himself up to sit on the wagon's tailgate.

" 'Hell hath no fury like a woman scorned,' " Matt said.

"Who said that?"

"Don't know."

"Who scorned her? She's married."

"She and Frank just had a session with the big boss," Matt said. "Apparently, the meeting didn't go her way. You know how Cody is—nice fella, but his say is final. He don't cotton to being told what to do, or how to do it."

Crowfoot waited for more.

"Annie's furious about Cody hiring that sharpshooter, Lillian Smith, and giving her equal billing." He paused to let the approving roar of 30,000 people recede.

"Little fat girl is good shot, but Annie is better," Crowfoot replied calmly, with barely a trace of his native accent. Straight from Pine Ridge Mission School to the Wild West Show two years earlier at the urging of retiring Sitting Bull, Crowfoot, at nineteen, was now a veteran performer. Leggings, beaded moccasins and fringed buckskin jacket were a perfect complement to his dark skin and

14

eagle feather woven into a scalplock—enough to fool any stranger into thinking him a bloodthirsty savage.

"Let's slip around the edge of the curtain and watch her," Matt suggested.

Matt and Crowfoot worked around to the back side where they wouldn't be noticed by the audience, and pulled back the canvas about a foot.

By this time, Annie had the spectators thoroughly warmed up. She rode her horse in a steady gallop in a wide circle around the arena. As they watched, she bent backward at the waist until she lay flat on the horse's rump. Raising the shotgun from her bouncing position, she shattered three clay pigeons Frank Butler fired into the air in quick succession with a hand trap.

The audience roared.

She tossed her .20 gauge to Frank as she passed him, then leapt off the horse, turning a somersault to break her momentum.

She selected a .22 Marlin rifle from the gun table, and Frank placed an apple on the head of her dog, the young St. Bernard, Sir Ralph. The dog sat stone still while Annie stepped off twenty paces, turned her back and cocked the rifle, resting it on her right shoulder, pointing backward. She held up a hand mirror in front of her and sighted into it for several seconds. The rifle cracked and the apple went flying in pulpy pieces.

"By damn!" Crowfoot muttered as the crowd went wild. "That woman is shooter!"

"She's automatic," Matt agreed. "Never misses. She has to miss now and then on purpose so the audience won't think her stunts are rigged."

They looked again and Annie was already into her next trick.

Frank was tossing silver dollars into the air, one at a time, then two at a time, then three. The rifle fire was unerring as the silver coins went spinning, struck by lead bullets.

The audience was roaring continuously now, drowning out everything else, including the popping of the gunshots. She faced the open end of the arena to be sure no bullets or lead shot landed in the grandstand.

Before the applause could die down, Annie and Frank worked quickly to set up three spring-loaded skeet traps on the ground. Annie took a few seconds to look around and Matt knew she was setting up the audience, pausing like a dramatic actress to get the spectators' full attention. The vast throng grew gradually silent, anticipating something big was about to happen.

Annie bent and set off the first, jumped to the second, then the third, and all three clay pigeons went arcing against the blue sky, one behind the other. In a flash of brown doeskin, she dashed to the gun table, turned a flip over it, snatched a pistol off the ground, lay prone and fired—*Bang! Bang! Bang!* The first, second and third discs exploded in a shower of clay fragments before they could fall, intact, to the ground. There was no containing the audience now. She could have declared herself Queen Victoria's successor, and everyone in that British audience would have approved.

"She's close to the end of her act," Matt said. "Let's get out of here. I don't want her to see me just now."

"I go on next," Crowfoot said, as the two of them headed toward the staging area. "I attack a helpless woman at sodbuster's cabin."

Dozens of Indians in traditional dress and war paint were milling around, talking and preparing their mounts for mock battle.

"Cody's nearly three times my age," Matt continued, picking up an earlier thought, "but he doesn't know a dime novel from a Bible if he thinks it's a good idea to hire a younger woman to compete with an older one." He shook his head at the painful ignorance of his elders. "A fifteen-year old who wears all her medals on her chest, shoots off her mouth…"

"A performer must have confidence," Crowfoot observed, running his hands down the flanks of his paint pony, and bending to check the unshod hooves.

"Annie's confident, but she's also very quiet and lady-like. She lets her guns do her bragging," Matt said.

"If she so confident, why does she now tell everyone she

twenty-two years old instead of twenty-eight?" the Indian asked.

Matt nodded. "Reckon she *is* running a little scared, no matter how well she's shooting."

Crowfoot nodded. "Females—human, wolf, buffalo, mountain lion—have instinct about such things. They do what they must to protect their young, their mates, their territory. For Annie, her position and her name."

"Fact is, Crofe, if Cody doesn't get rid of Lillian Smith, I'm afraid Annie and Frank'll quit the show. Then where will *I* be? Feeding and watering the buffaloes and shoveling manure?"

"You already doing that," Crowfoot grinned. "Maybe Cody make you Lillian's errand boy."

Matt let the horror of that image sink in. "Whew! She's nearly two years younger than I am. And she's used to getting her way. I didn't hire on to baby sit a spoiled brat."

Crowfoot straightened up. "You same as me—hired on to do what the boss tells you. You and I not big and strong to be roustabouts, not good shooters to be marksmen, not horsemen to be trick riders, not rich to be owners. Your God—or my Great Spirit—made me Indian and that's what I play in this show." He looked at Matt with obsidian eyes. "When Annie just a little girl, Captain Adam Bogardus was world champion marksman. Ten years ago, the great Doc Carver challenge him for top spot. Bogardus win and was bright light of this show. But time goes like the big river," he made a flowing motion with his arm, "and drowned the steamboat with all Bogardus's guns and gear. Just then, Annie asks for job. Manager, Nate Salsbury, sees her perform and hires her on the spot. Borgardus goes from big man to nobody, just like that." Crowfoot made a chopping motion with the edge of his hand. "All things have their season. I will know when the day comes for me to live other lives and change from Crowfoot to my white mission name, Frank Thomas."

"Yeah, reckon I need to make the most of every minute I live. I'm lucky to have any job with this show. Being a gun boy for the great and famous Annie Oakley will be something I can tell my grandkids someday."

Popping of rapid gunfire from the arena indicated Annie's show had reached its climax.

"You know," Matt said, thoughtfully, "you speak better English than most whites in this show. I think you were born to speak our language, rather than Sioux."

"I make English my language," Crowfoot said. "To speak and write like whites will be good later. I always be Sioux, but must be ready to move on. Too many Sioux stay on reservation and get drunk, then die."

The huge crowd erupted into thunderous applause as Annie skipped out of the arena and the canvas curtain fell behind her.

"My turn," Crowfoot said, vaulting onto his pony's back and urging him up toward the entrance with a dozen other Sioux riders.

CHAPTER 3

Inspector Abberline sat in the Three Bells public house, nursing a pint of bitters. It was his favorite drink, but tonight he hardly tasted it as he stared into space, oblivious to the noise and bustle around him.

It'd been just a week since the murder of Polly Nichols. For some reason, he'd been drawn to her funeral yesterday at the City of London Cemetery in Ilford. There'd been no real reason for him to attend—nothing more he could learn there. Perhaps he was hoping the murderer would show up anonymously among the mourners who were few enough in number and included her father, her husband and her eldest son, along with several of her friends from her more recent life in Whitechapel. Police and the undertaker had worked together to stave off the idly curious and the morbid from attending, so the cortege could pass unhindered.

Abberline had stood near the open grave while a Church of England priest, wearing a white surplice over his black robe, read the burial service. Abberline glanced at the faces of the few mourners, wondering what they were thinking. The man who'd been pointed out to him by the clergyman as the father stood bareheaded, thinning hair ruffling in the slight breeze. His sunken cheeks made him look as if he might fall into a heap any second beneath the black topcoat. What a blow this must be to a parent, Abberline thought, to have a child end up like this. The estranged husband, wearing a threadbare tweed jacket too small for his bulky torso stood, stony faced. He was probably attending because he felt obligated as the legal spouse, rather than out of any sense of love. Mere speculation on my part, Abberline reprimanded himself. The man might very well be broken hearted. Certainly that was the look conveyed by the face of the grown son who appeared to be in his late twenties. Lean and dark haired, a haunting sense of grief showed in the hollowed-eyed look the young man turned on the plain pine box.

"…we hereby commit the body of our sister to the earth in sure and certain hope of the resurrection…" the priest intoned. He reached forward, grasping a handful of fresh loam from the mound of dirt and sprinkling it over the wooden lid of the casket that had been lowered into the open grave. Each of the family members did the same, in turn, followed by a half-dozen women friends who stood in a group to one side. Abberline recognized Beth Hampton, Liz Stride and Catherine Eddowes among them. Nothing could sound more final than the hollow thumping of those dirt clods on the lid of that coffin, Abberline thought, a lump forming in his throat.

As he put on his hat and turned away, he took another good look at those attending. Four men were strangers to him. But their age and general appearance told him there was not even a remote chance any of them could be suspected of being the killer. Not that he had any idea what the killer looked like. Yet, his experience and investigative instincts told him the man was lithe and strong, not over middle age. It had to be someone who was quick on his feet, not overweight, would not stand out in an East End crowd, and probably had strong hands—perhaps those of a workingman, instead of a gentleman.

He was glad he came, even if he learned nothing further that would help him solve this case. It was good to realize that these prostitutes were not just names and post-mortem reports. They had backgrounds. They'd been real people, with real interests, feelings, loves, and hopes. They'd started life in very different ways. This woman had married, and had at least one child. He wondered what'd gone wrong. He'd glean some knowledge of her past from the inquest and from the statements of her friends. He was always curious about the route each of the women he knew had taken to wind up on the street. And now this one had come to a brutal, violent end. His was not to judge, but to learn the facts and to ponder the realization that bad situations, flawed judgment and human weaknesses could do in even the best person.

In spite of intensive effort, widespread questioning of potential witnesses, searches of the neighborhood, along with tips and suggestions from the public, the police were no closer to identifying the slasher than they'd been the night of the murder. Not only that, but the authorities were left with only guesswork as to his motivation.

Abberline sipped his beer. Being an investigator could be a frustrating business. Many man hours and much legwork had been spent by the police, to no avail. They'd eliminated many people, but this had not led to a narrowing of possibilities. Conversely, the list of suspects seemed to be growing daily.

He sat back in his chair with a sigh, debating whether to order a steak and kidney pie. Often he thought better on a full stomach. The Three Bells was justly famous for the flaky crusts on its kidney pies. Nothing soggy here. He signaled for the serving girl. "Kidney pie, Caroline," he said. "A fresh one if you please. Not heated."

"You're a lucky man, inspector." She flashed him a smile as she wiped her hands on her apron.

Pretty girl. Only one tooth missing that he could see.

"Robert took four from the oven not three hours ago. And there's just one left."

"And another pint to go with it." He held up his glass to show the remaining bitters.

She brought the pie and refilled his glass. They knew each other well, and he would have loved to give a pat to that nice round rump as she turned away, but thought better of it. Maybe she could sit on his lap while he questioned her about the murder. That wouldn't do, either. He was too well known and respected around here to start anything like that. Clacking tongues about his alleged liaisons would do nothing to enchance his reputation. Besides, Caroline

21

had been thoroughly questioned by the police and could offer no useful information. He must keep everything professional. But, damnation, there was nothing else to go on. That's why his mind was wandering. As he savored the pie and the beer, he gradually came to the conclusion that Polly Nichols' murder was most likely an anomaly committed by some itinerant, maybe a sailor passing through the port, crazed by too much drink, or by a long hatred of women, or by the green dragon—a one time act of violence by a demented man long gone.

He watched the patrons filing in and out of the smoky room. Although he frequented other pubs in Whitechapel, the Three Bells was his favorite. He'd come to know the regulars by sight and many by name—night watchmen, laborers on the docks, carmen—workers whose jobs required them to be abroad at odd hours. He also knew the bartenders, the serving girls, the prostitutes.

In spite of the week-old murder of the Nichols woman and the two killings preceding that, he could detect no apprehension, no panic among the women who habitually gathered at this pub between customers. Over the foamy rim of his glass, he observed four women at a nearby table. In reality they were probably much younger than they appeared at a glance. They were in a jolly mood and he caught a few words of some ribald joke. Three of the women laughed aloud. The fourth, known as "Dark Annie" Chapman only pulled her shawl around her and frowned at her empty glass. Annie's dark moods had given her the cognomen, along with her black hair and eyes.

"Annie, you're a riot!" Mary Kelly cried, throwing her head back until her wavy auburn hair cascaded over her shoulders. Of the group, she was the youngest and prettiest, and likely the most popular. Her lilting Irish tongue and free, generous spirit—even in lean times—made her a great favorite among those of both sexes. Abberline wondered what kind of background she'd come from in Ireland.

"It's the way she tells them—deadpan," laughed Liz Stride. She was only five feet five, but nicknamed "Long Liz" because of

22

her last name, "Stride". A plain-looking woman, she could have been anywhere from thirty-five to forty-five. "Tell us true, now, did he really say that, or did you make it up?'

They whooped with laughter again, and several heads at the bar turned in their direction.

They were all dressed in long, full dresses, two of them wearing men's overcoats and Annie a heavy shawl to ward off the September chill.

To Abberline's discerning eye the clothing was worn and threadbare, castoffs they'd picked up here and there at lodging houses and second hand stores, augmented now and then with something reasonably new.

The time was less than half ten, early in their working day, so none of the four seemed to be in her cups.

"Tom, bring us a gin, will ya, luv?" Dark Annie called to a lean, mustachioed bartender who was passing their table, tray in hand.

"Best go easy on that, Annie," Mary Jane Kelly cautioned. "Don't want to be spendin' your doss money before you earn it."

Dark Annie, shifted her short, somewhat stout figure in the chair. "Don't worry, Mary, this is my last one. I'm takin' these liver pills they give me at the infirmary. They said no more than two drinks a night while the pills lasted."

"Two drinks a night, is it?" a woman with a straw hat pinned to her mousy brown hair said. "You must be workin' on next Thursday's quota."

The three of them burst into laughter.

"Really, Annie, if you're a bit poorly, you might want to lay off a few nights and rest, especially if there's some crazy on the streets."

" 'Lay off a few nights', she says." Annie assumed a mocking tone. "If I was one of Queen Vic's ladies-in-waitin', I could probably do just that. As for the crazy on the street, he's likely off to parts unknown by now. The police been sweepin' clean as a broom since poor Polly left us. They haven't found tic or whisper of 'im."

She accepted her small glass of gin from the waiter and took a generous gulp. "If I run across this gent tonight, I'll give his willie such a twist, he'll think it's a pretzel."

"Seriously, Annie, you need to have a caution."

"I will." She pushed back her chair. "Hmmm…that gin doesn't seem to be settin' well on m'stomach tonight. You can finish it. I'd best be off. I don't want to be at it 'til daylight." She pushed back her dark, wavy hair, and moved toward the door, appearing a bit unsteady on her feet.

"Poor thing, she's 'ad too much already."

"Don't think so," Mary said. "I been here a few hours with 'er. She didn't drink that much. I think she's sick."

Abberline watched her go, feeling a familiar twinge of pity. These women— the ignored, the unknown—who'd sunk toward the bottom of society's ladder, were taking great risks. They dealt every night with strangers, many of them rough men, drunk, some violent. And their recompense was a few coins to buy a bed in a lodging house, a meal and a gin. From what he knew of their personal histories, many of them had started out with little. Through bad choices, lack of saleable skills, abusive husbands, or just bad luck, they'd wound up here, selling themselves until they died early of diseases.

A firm rap on the door of his flat brought Abberline awake instantly from a light sleep. He rolled over in the dark, rubbing his eyes. "Yes?"

"Corporal Carnes," a voice from the hallway answered.

"One moment." He swung his legs over the side of the bed, stomach tensing with that familiar apprehension that always came with an alarm in the night.

He hadn't slept well. The meat pie lay heavy on his stomach. He pulled on his trousers, looped up the braces, and swung a shirt around his shoulders. From long habit of caution, he pulled his Adams from the holster on the bedpost.

A draft of cold air rushed in as he shot the bolt and opened the door six inches. A low-burning lamp in the hallway showed a muscular uniformed policeman.

"Sorry to disturb you at this hour, Inspector."

"Quite all right. What's the problem?"

"There's been another murder in Whitechapel."

"A prostitute?"

"Yes, sir. Even worse than before."

"Let me dress. Won't be a minute."

"There's a Hansom waiting."

Closing the door, he fumbled for a match on the bedside table. Striking it, he lit the lamp and picked up his watch—6:14 a.m.

Gray daylight illuminated the scene when they pulled up in front of a lodging house at 29 Hanbury Street.

At the edge of a loose cluster of people, Doctor Andrew Llewellyn was talking to a constable.

"Doctor, you always seem to arrive ahead of me," Abberline said by way of greeting.

"They call me first because I'm close by. Half the time I sleep on a cot in my surgery. But they needn't have been in a rush. She's been dead for at least an hour."

"Same as before?"

The doctor nodded. "Come and see."

The door on the ground floor of the big frame house stood ajar and Abberline saw it opened into a passageway that led all the way through to the back door. He followed the doctor and a constable who carried a lantern. The back door opened out into a yard enclosed by a board fence that separated the yard from the adjoining property. They went through a gate and the clump of police and neighbors parted to let them in. Someone had partially covered the body with a large grain sack, leaving the feet, encased in high-top shoes, sticking out from beneath. Abberline took the lantern from the constable, bracing himself for what was to come. He bent and

25

pulled off the sack. A woman lay on her back, petticoats bunched up above the knees. What appeared to be the small intestines and attachments were pulled out and draped over the right shoulder. Part of the stomach, tissue and skin with pubic hair was draped over the left shoulder. The bullseye reflected from the mass of bright blood at her throat. He tilted the beam up slightly to see her face. Black, wavy hair, and a pug nose. It was Dark Annie Chapman.

Abberline put the stained grain sack back over the sight and straightened up, shuttering the lantern.

"You say this happened only an hour ago?"

"Give or take," the doctor said. "I thought longer at first. But the massive loss of blood, plus the chilly air, made the body cool down quickly."

The two men moved away to talk privately.

"Her name is Annie Chapman. I saw her leave the Three Bells last night at half after ten. We need to question anyone who might have seen her later. I heard her say she wouldn't be soliciting until daylight because she was ill and wanted to earn just enough for her doss." He turned to his friend. "But all that is police work—not your concern."

They paused by the corner of the fence in the gray morning light. Abberline almost wished darkness still covered this dreary scene. "Tell me what you saw that I missed."

"Swollen tongue and throat bruises consistent with strangulation, just as before. Probably choked to unconsciousness to prevent struggles while he slashed her throat. Abrasions on the fingers, as if rings were forcibly removed."

"I can't imagine she had any rings worth stealing," Abberline said. "Disemboweled like the Nichols woman."

"Yes, but some of the organs are entirely missing."

"Missing?"

"That's correct, unless they turn up in a trash can or were tossed somewhere nearby. We'll know after a search. Part of the stomach wall, including the navel, the womb, upper part of the vagina and most of the bladder are gone."

"Why would he do that?"

Doctor Llewellyn shrugged his broad shoulders. "There's no logic to this; but the way the cutting was done suggests some anatomical knowledge."

Abberline arched his brows.

"Doesn't appear to be only a random, frenzied slashing. And the positioning of the inner organs—why not leave them where they fell?"

His question hung unanswered in the subdued light of dawn.

"I'll make a thorough exam at the morgue, but I believe the knife used had a blade six to eight inches long, thin and sharp."

A shiver ran up Abberline's back, as if an icy breath had blown on the back of his neck. Needing to shake off the eerie sensation, he moved to one side and pointed. "Blood was smeared on the fence, so apparently she was killed here."

"Just as before," the doctor agreed. "A secluded spot, away from view of the street."

Abberline inhaled deeply. "Do you have the feeling we've done all this before, a week ago?"

"Detail for detail."

"Well, no need for me to come to the infirmary with you this time," he said. "I'll get your autopsy report tomorrow. Think I'll stay here and help the police search and question possible witnesses."

"Very good. I'll be in touch." Doctor Llewellyn nodded and walked away.

Abberline watched as the doctor directed the police to lift the body to a stretcher for removal to the makeshift morgue.

When the remains of Dark Annie were gone, he walked back inside the fenced yard and listened as the constables interviewed the landlady who owned the property. Neither she nor her boarders had heard a thing. Not unusual. He moved on to another policeman who was taking notes and talking to three young men.

Abberline perked up his ears.

"Yes…that's right, officer. My name's John Richardson. I'm the son of the landlady, Mrs. Amelia Richardson."

"And what did you see?"

"Nothing. I don't live here, but I come by often to check on the house because my mother leaves this passageway open on the ground floor. I came here this morning about 4:30 on my way to market. Went through the passage and stood on the steps leading into the back yard."

"And…?" The constable was becoming impatient.

"I stopped to cut a piece of leather off my boot that was chafing my foot. Then I left, but I didn't see or hear anything."

"What about you, Mister…?"

"Albert Cadosh. I live next door at 27 Hanbury Street. I came out about 5:30 and heard some conversation from behind the fence separating our two yards."

"What did they say?"

"They were talking low and all I hard was a woman saying 'No'. I walked back into the house and then came out again about three or four minutes later. That's when I heard something fall heavily against the fence."

"And you didn't bother to take a look?"

"What goes on in the Richardson's yard is none of my business."

The constable turned to the third man. "You found the body?"

"Yes. I'm a boarder here, and I came out about 6:00. It was nearly daylight then, and I found her lying just as you saw. Nothing much else to say. I ran next door and hollered at the two men working at the packing case manufacturer. They came and looked, then went for the police."

Abberline drifted away as the constable was making notes. Except for the killer, these were the closest witnesses to the crime. Their statements confirmed the time and place of the murder, but nothing else. Perhaps an examination of the body would yield some clues.

But the post mortem gave no further leads to identifying the killer.

Abberline read Dr. Llewellyn's report, and also attended most of the inquest that was scattered over the next five days. Annie's friends came to testify, and he learned a few more details, but nothing significant. Near the body the police had found part of an envelope, a pocket comb, and two polished farthings. It was a popular con trick to polish farthings so, in dim light, they could be passed for shillings.

A wet leather apron was found a few rods from the body in the yard, but it turned out to be a work apron of one of the boarders. The apron had been washed and hung to dry.

The torn envelope with a partial address was thought at first to be a clue. But Tim Donovan, landlord of Annie's lodging house, said he saw her pick up the envelope from the floor and tear off a corner to hold her liver pills. Donovan said Annie was sitting in the kitchen just after midnight because she didn't have money for a bed. Then she went out for a pint of beer with one of the lodgers and returned, apparently drunk, at 1:35 where she again sat in the kitchen, eating a baked potato. "I told her she always seemed to have money for drink, but not for a bed," Donovan testified.

John Evans, the night watchman at the boarding house, said as she left again, she told him, "I won't be long, Brummy. See that Tim keeps the bed for me while I get m'doss money."

The best testimony came from one Elizabeth Darrell who saw Chapman at 5:30 a.m. outside 29 Hanbury Street, talking to a man. Darrell described him as being over forty, "a bit foreign looking, wearing a deerstalker hat and a dark coat. He'd a shabby, genteel appearance, if y'know what I mean. I 'eard 'im ask Annie, 'Will you?' and she said, 'Yes.'"

Later, in the Three Bells, Abberline sifted through notes he'd taken during the inquest and facts the doctor had given him concerning the autopsy. Most of it was useless. Over the years, he'd found witnesses' statements, however well-intentioned, to be mostly inaccurate. "Facts" sworn to usually proved to be wildly erroneous and unreliable. Most people were not trained observers, and the memory played tricks.

But the vague description of the man seen by Elizabeth Darrell—*that* was the likely killer. If only she'd seen his face!

CHAPTER 4

GHASTLY MURDER blared the headline of *THE STAR*, the two-word headline covering half the front page. "Whitechapel Prostitutes Gutted Like Fish" was in slightly smaller type below, and then, "Fourth Slashing Has Police Baffled." The column descended with further details in smaller type.

Abberline tossed the folded paper down on his desk. He expected such outbursts from the *STAR* and other tabloids, like the *ILLUSTRATED POLICE NEWS*, whose existence depended on an unending string of sensational stories.

Yet, a somewhat saner newspaper, the *DAILY TELEGRAPH*, ran a headline, DEMENTED SLASHER ROAMS EAST END. Even the more sedate *LONDON TIMES* carried the story of Annie Chapman's murder as front page news, summarizing the three previous murders the police suspected were committed by the same individual.

The three newspapers were several days old, but the current editions all carried follow-up stories. Now that the public had been sufficiently alarmed, the Letters to the Editor sections of these papers had been expanded to accommodate dozens of outcries from writers. Jews were blamed, foreigners were blamed, a spurned lover was blamed, butchers in the Whitechapel district were blamed, recent insane asylum inmates were blamed. Abberline knew the papers were publishing only some of the less offensive letters. He'd seen many others that flooded into police headquarters, and concluded

31

London had more than its share of people teetering on a knife edge of reality—people tipped over into their own delusional world by published details of mutilations.

Letter writers offered hundreds of theories of who might have done it and the reasons why—some very bizarre reasons, indeed. Those citizens who were offering their own suspects or solutions, were complaining the law was not doing enough to catch the killer. They predicted when and where he might strike again. Even those who'd probably never set foot in Whitechapel wailed about being in mortal danger. Reading dozens of these letters had made his skin crawl nearly as much as looking at the slasher's victims.

Working in the CID, the Crime Investigation Division of Scotland Yard, Abberline had a very public job, and everyone, it seemed, wanted to tell him how to do it.

He sighed, staring out the window where rain was streaking the coal dust on the wavy glass. It might be a different story if the Metropolitan London Police, Scotland Yard, and all the various divisions of each, functioned as a cohesive unit. But, in such a bureaucracy, that rarely happened. The heads of divisions and departments were often men who carried knighthoods and had the ear of the Queen or the Prime Minister. Their primary job was making themselves look good in public. If they began to appear incompetent, they were let go in disgrace. These men would do nearly anything to maintain their good public image.

A discreet rap on his office door.

Abberline swiveled in his chair. "Come in."

The door opened and his clerk, a slender man in an impeccable black suit, said, "Sir Charles would like to see you, sir."

"Very well. I'll be there directly."

The door closed.

Abberline got up and straightened his tie in the dim reflection of his bookcase glass. He'd been expecting this. Charles Warren was Metropolitan Police Commissioner, two steps up the ladder from his immediate boss, Sir Robert Anderson, Head of CID. But, when summoned, one didn't take refuge in the chain of command.

Striding down the hall, he choked back the nausea that made him feel as if he'd swallowed a live squid. He was angry with himself. With his age and experience, he shouldn't be having qualms like a rookie.

He was shown into Warren's private office by his secretary who closed the door quietly as he left. Heavy woodwork and thick carpet deadened all outside sounds. He stood at a distance in front of the massive desk, until Sir Charles looked up and stacked some papers aside. "Have a seat," he said, pointing at a horsehair padded straight chair a few feet away.

Warren remained standing behind the desk, looking down at him.

"Have you seen what the newspapers are saying?" The man seemed to wear a permanent frown. Abberline couldn't recall ever seeing him smile.

"Yessir."

"Some of them are calling for my resignation."

"I haven't seen that. But there will always be malcontents in the press, sir."

"Yes, one can't put much stock in what they say. They're in business to sell papers, after all. What I want to know is why these reporters are allowed to trail around after the police and interview the same witnesses who've just been questioned."

Without giving Abberline a chance to answer, he went on. "The Police Department gives them the pertinent facts and that's what they should print. Instead, they flock into the inquests and procure the most lurid details which they use in their sensational pieces, further stirring up a very gullible public."

He paused and glared at Abberline, who felt compelled to say something. "I don't mean to be impertinent, sir, but it's a free country. We can't stop them from interviewing anyone who'll talk to them. And most witnesses are just ordinary folk who like the attention, like to see themselves in print. As for the inquests…"

"I know, I know," Warren interrupted with a wave of his hand. "They're open to the public."

Abberline kept silent while Warren picked up a stack of letters from his desk.

"It's not just the newspapers, either. Hundreds of letters are pouring in to the department, many of them from dangerous cranks." He sifted through the stack in front of him. "Here's one who complains the law is blaming him for the murders and signs it with the initials, J.C., which the context of the letter makes clear, stands for Jesus Christ." He dropped it and picked up another. "This man claims the killer is using a chloroform-soaked handkerchief to stupefy his victims before killing them. Therefore, anyone who comes near a woman and appears to be blowing his nose should be arrested."

Abberline had to bite his lip to keep from smiling.

"Here's another who suggests the killer might be using an old vault in the Jews' Cemetery as a hiding place. Another says the killer could be disappearing suddenly by using the underground sewers. Here's a man who says the prostitutes' clothing should be sprayed with a syringe of corrosive liquid so that when the next victim is found, her killer could be traced by means of this material on his clothing.

"And these are not the most bizarre. One or two claim to be the killer, himself, but they're thought to be crackpots." He gripped a fistful of letters as he came around the desk. "Here's one." He slipped a letter out of the stack. "He advocates that all the whores be protected from strangulation by being fitted with barbed collars, or collars made of flexible metal that would be electrically charged by being wired to a small battery. He proposes something like chain mail for the body to prevent slashing."

Abberline didn't reply, but was of the opinion this last idea might have some merit.

Warren paused, searching the letters in his hand. Abberline sat quietly, not wanting to open further avenues of discussion. He'd let the boss have his say and purge his frustrations.

"Here's one," Warren said. "It's from an English teacher who's been abroad for the past twenty-two years. He suggests the killer might be a follower of Buddha, one of the Thugs who are experienced killers and feel bound to offer human sacrifice to their deity. He thinks maybe the murders taking place at certain times of the month are coinciding with human sacrifice that must match certain phases of the moon." He dropped the letter on his desk and selected another from his handful. "Here's a writer who thinks the killer might have traveled in China and come in contact with an Oriental custom. He states a man afflicted with syphilis sometimes uses the part cut off from the woman as a kind of poultice to draw the virus from his ulcers. This correspondent claims that Chinese criminals murder women for this very purpose."

"There are all manner of theories," Abberline interjected as Warren glanced over several more sheets of paper in his voluminous correspondence. "I have seen several dozen letters from the public," he continued, filling the gap in Warren's monologue. "I'm sure all these people who took the time and interest to write us are expressing what they believe to be very helpful suggestions that could aid us in solving the case."

"And they think the police are stupid for not following up on their advice, no matter how strange it may seem to a reasonable person," Warren said. "I won't bore you with too many of these, but I just want to share with you some of the public reaction to our failure to make an arrest in this case." He drew forth a long sheet covered with a bold scrawl. He tilted the letter toward the light from the window. "This writer suggests the killer might be an Indian hill tribesman because, in Sanscrit mythology, special reverence is given to male and female genital organs. This man says he's been informed by old soldiers who have inside knowledge of the practice that the organs themselves are preserved and hung up or worn as amulets, and so forth. He speculates there might be some members of these people operating in the East End. Physically, they'd blend in with any other Europeans on the streets. Even worse, he says the killer might be some old white soldier who's suffered sunstroke in India and adopted the barbaric customs of the hill tribes, killing these prostitutes to obtain their sexual organs."

Warren shook his head. "He goes on to say that this same old soldier/informant had told him it was common for East Indians to carry a concealed weapon with a fine needle point dipped in poison. Anyone pricked with this needle or sharp thorn, would be dead within seconds. He says that a man armed with such a weapon could, while caressing a woman, easily prick her neck or spine, causing her to collapse dead in his arms, and then could slash her throat to divert suspicion from the ritualistic poison murder. The removal of the female organs would be considered by the authorities as just part of the overall gashing."

"Sir, some of the public sincerely want to help, while others… well…are mentally unbalanced. There are any number of deranged individuals out there who are very capable of such acts. That's what makes narrowing down the suspects so much more difficult."

Warren waved a hand at the pile of letters on his desk. "Yes. There are those on the edge of mental collapse who've been sent into a frenzy by all the publicity. Their minds cannot deal with the details of gore the newspapers are feeding them on a daily basis. Several writers suggest the killer is attempting to overthrow the government of the Empire by thwarting the law enforcement establishment and making them look ridiculous." He suddenly noticed the lone letter he still held. "Oh, yes, here's one you'll like. This man suggests we run an electric wire along the curbstones with an alarm button attached at thirty-foot intervals. This alarm wire would be connected to all the stores and public houses where constables stop to warm themselves on cold winter nights. Then, when a prostitute is attacked and pushes an alarm button, a constable can pick out the location by the color-coded button that lights up. All constables should be mounted, he says, so they can gallop to the rescue in a hurry."

Warren sighed. "One of the less costly suggestions is from a man who wants locks of hair from the victims because he has a friend who can track down the killer by the prostitutes' hair. This friend, he says, has somehow found men who were guilty of animal cruelty by a psychic use of the animal hair."

"It's too bad the police must waste so many hours reading

all these to decide which merit a follow-up, but there's no help for that," Abberline said.

"More to the point, Home Secretary, Henry Matthews, and even Her Majesty are taking an interest in all this. It is no longer just a sordid police matter." He paused, staring at a far corner of the room. Then he turned to Abberline. "Did you know there were eighty murders in the city of London last year, yet not one of them was done in Whitechapel?"

"Remarkable."

"Remarkable, indeed, considering it's the poorest, most densely packed slum in the city. The residents must do whatever they can just to survive. Yet now, within a few weeks, there have been at least four murders there, of the most horrible type, at least two of which are undoubtedly by the same man."

"We are doing everything humanly possible to track him down, sir."

"Sir Robert Anderson, head of CID, and Sir James Fraser, Commissioner of the City of London Police tell me the same thing. They've committed a vast majority of their force to this investigation. But it's not enough. We must have an arrest."

Abberline was beginning to perspire under his waistcoat, even though the room was cool enough. Why was Sir Charles telling him all this? Did he have something in mind? "Sir, in more than twenty years of detective work, I've noticed that a killer will eventually make a mistake, and leave a pertinent clue, or do something to trip himself up. Even brilliant criminals are not perfect. This man may be some sort of unbalanced genius, but he cannot go on committing such violent dissections in the midst of a crowded part of the city, without being discovered. Sometimes pure happenstance and luck play a part. I sincerely believe we will catch him before long."

"That all sounds very reassuring, but when? Even Home Secretary Matthews is demanding action."

Abberline didn't know how to respond. Demanding such a thing was as impossible as ordering him to actually invent one of Jules Verne's imaginary flying machines. One could demand all he wished, but that wasn't going to make it happen.

"The reason I'm saying this is to impress upon you the gravity of the situation. And…if you can think of any unconventional method that might be useful in trapping this killer," he said, "*use it.*" He rubbed a hand across the thick mustache that nearly hid his mouth, then went back behind his desk and sat down. "As for me, I'm going to try a more conventional approach. If there is still some sort of scent remaining on the last victim's clothing, it's possible we can use bloodhounds to track it. I'll be conducting an experiment in Hyde Park before long to find out. In the meantime, you're free to use your experience and imagination to match wits with this slasher." His dark eyes bored into Abberline's. "*Take whatever action you think necessary to rid us of this pestilence.*" The words were emphatic and directed to him—not through the chain of command—but at him, personally.

"Yessir." He got up. "Thank you, sir." He bowed slightly and moved toward the door.

Walking back to his office he unbuttoned his coat and breathed a sigh of relief. Talks like that were never pleasant, but Sir Charles was clearly giving him a veiled signal to break the rules, if any, to apprehend the killer. Charles Warren wanted him to act outside conventional police work, if he thought it would accomplish the task of capturing or killing this man.

But that put Abberline, himself, on an island. If he did something completely weird—and somehow managed to trap the slasher—Warren would take the credit as a brilliant tactician. If—as seemed more likely—Abberline tried something that only resulted in more murders, or embarrassment to the department, Warren would conveniently forget they'd ever had such a conversation, and Abberline would likely be fired.

He wondered again why he hadn't taken his mother's advice years ago and become a country parson.

CHAPTER 5

"Andrew, I feel like a jackdaw among swans." Abberline tugged at his stiff collar and glanced self-consciously at the elegantly-dressed men and women milling about on the greensward.

"Nonsense, Fred," Doctor Llewellyn said, guiding him by the elbow toward the shade of some trees where a long table was set with all manner of fancy hors d'oeuvres. "I'm a member of this shooting club and you're my guest." He ladled up a crystal cup full of mint green punch from a silver bowl. "Here… I know you'd prefer a glass of bitters, but I think you'll find this tasty."

Abberline took the cup and sipped—a delicious, minty concoction spiked with something alcoholic.

"The exhibition will start in about ten minutes."

Abberline nodded, taking another swallow of the delightful punch. He plucked a meat and cheese hors d'oeuvre by its toothpick from one of several dozen bowls on the snow-white linen. "Certainly beats pickled eggs and rat trap cheese in the Three Bells. Maybe if I get outside two more cups of this punch, I'll be able to relax."

"We both need to get away from our work for a day now and then," Llewellyn said as they strolled out into the sunshine. He drew a deep breath. "Lovely day."

A dreary downpour of rain had finally ceased three days before. "Without a good sluicing now and again, Whitechapel would be even dirtier than it is," Abberline said.

"Huh! That goes for the rest of London as well," the doctor

39

replied, pulling a flat cigar case from the pocket of his tattersall vest. "At least out here, away from the city, there's not so much coal smoke and soot."

Abberline finished his small cup of punch, and was ready for another. He could scarcely believe he was surrounded by such opulence. This was a different world—the world of the privileged upper class, lawn parties and organized sporting events. If he inhabited this level of society, would he have the energy and creativity to work at spending unlimited pounds and filling unlimited time? The swarming East End labored and lusted, sweated and swore to maintain a miserable existence only a few miles from here. But it might have been on the Indian sub-continent, the contrast was so sharp.

Sir Charles Warren had talked to him eight days ago. It seemed like a month. Nothing had changed. The killer was still at large. Abberline had not come up with any new ideas to trap the deadly phantom. Yet, there'd been no frenzied slashings in more than a fortnight. Whitechapel prostitutes, sometimes traveling in pairs, were cautiously returning to the gaslit cobblestones and shadowy byways. Maybe it was all over.

"None of that today, my friend," Doctor Llewellyn said.

"What?" Abberline was jarred out of his reverie.

"I saw that look on your face. You were thinking about those murders. While you're here today, you will enjoy yourself. That's an order. No worry, no wondering—not even any thinking about work. Understand?"

Abberline relaxed and smiled. "Agreed."

Llewellyn struck a match and cupped a hand against the slight breeze to light his cigar. A few early Fall leaves fluttered down around them. "Most of these people," he continued, gesturing with the lighted stogie, "know I'm a doctor of some sort, but only a few close friends have any idea what I really do for a living." He gave a tight smile and smoothed his mustache. "I daresay, some of the more delicate ladies would be shocked if they saw me in my other life—up to my elbows in blood."

They moved back to the table and Abberline refilled his cup.

The doctor consulted his heavy gold watch. "Time for us to get a good seat."

They fell in with the crowd drifting toward the open ground on the far side of the trees. A set of bleachers accommodated most of the two hundred plus in attendance. The rest reclined on a slope of grass in the sunshine where they could get a good view of the broad field. The several acres of the East Sycamore Gun Club were encompassed by a low stone wall. The pitched roof and chimney of the clubhouse were visible in a distant grove.

"Have you attended Cody's Wild West Show?" the doctor asked as they slid into the second row of the temporary stands.

"No. Honestly, that type of entertainment doesn't appeal to me. Give me an occasional music hall performance."

"Completely different," the doctor said. "I've always been fascinated by the American West—a new, raw country. As a man who carries a pistol in performance of his duty, you know something of firearms. I think you'll appreciate what you're about to witness."

"So you've been to the show?"

"Oh, yes—twice," Llewellyn said. "It didn't take any effort on my part to persuade the president of this club to invite Annie Oakley to put on a shooting exhibition here."

Abberline recalled the faded wall poster he'd seen in Whitechapel trumpeting 'Buffalo Bill and his Congress of Rough Riders of the World', commonly referred to in the papers as 'Bill Cody's Wild West Show'. "Is this young lady really as good as the newspapers make her out to be?"

"Better." Llewellyn removed the cigar from his mouth and flicked off the ash.

Abberline knew his friend was not given to hyperbole.

"Cody's show also features a 15-year old California girl who's quite a marksman as well."

"Is she here, too?"

The doctor shook his head. "She was invited to the Wimbledon Shooting Grounds this summer and had a miserable day trying to shoot those iron running deer targets. In fact, she was fined for hitting several of them in the haunch. She left the grounds in a huff without paying the fine."

Abberline looked his question as his friend.

"Shooting a real deer in the haunch is disgraceful for a hunter. It's worse than a miss because the deer isn't killed and just runs off and dies slowly from the wound."

"Well, shooting's a big sport in England but I carry my Adams only for close range defense." He didn't add that shooting birds or clay pigeons with a shotgun or rifle—while good for sharpening hand/eye coordination—held no appeal for him.

While they talked, the last of the equipment was being put in place by members of the club—stationary and hand-held spring traps, a variety of clay pigeons, and glass balls, caged "blue rocks"— the lightning fast English birds that were used as live targets.

The doctor pointed at a lean man in a wide brimmed hat who was directing the positioning of everything, including the table that held a variety of long guns and ammunition. "Frank Butler, Annie's husband and manager."

The crowd applauded politely as if awaiting the beginning of a lawn tennis match. Annie appeared, removed a wide hat and placed it on the table, then curtsied to the crowd in the stands, only forty feet away. She was dressed in a long sleeved beige blouse, a pleated, fringed skirt and doeskin leggings. Her chestnut hair was tied back, but still hung past her shoulders. As she worked off her fitted gloves, Abberline gauged her height at no more than five feet, one inch. Petite, but athletic, he guessed. Under thirty years old— straight nose, full lips, and very pretty.

"Makes her own clothes, I hear," a lady sitting nearby said in a stage whisper.

For the next three-quarters of an hour, the audience witnessed a display of marksmanship that made even the skeptical Abberline, gasp with amazement. With hardly a break between each, Annie started with a short exhibition of shooting a .22 rifle. Then she switched to a short shotgun and shot two clay pigeons Frank sprang from a hand trap. Then she pulled the trap herself, snatched the gun and fired. Then she stood with her back to the trap, turned and fired.

But this was just a warm-up. She next waited until the trap was sprung, grabbed her shotgun from the ground and fired, breaking the clay pigeon. Then she repeated this trick with two clay pigeons. Standing twenty feet from the gun, she waited until the trap was sprung before she ran, snatched the weapon and fired. Then she held a ball in one hand, tossed it up and fired, breaking it. The trick was repeated, but she threw two balls into the air and hit them both. Between each, Frank Butler announced to the crowd what she was about to do, since her movements were so rapid, the eye could hardly follow.

The tricks grew more difficult. She threw a ball backward, over her shoulder, picked up the gun, whirled and fired. She broke six balls thrown into the air in four seconds. She broke five balls in five seconds, first with a rifle, then repeated the trick twice more, using two different shotguns.

As a finale, she was challenged to a shooting contest by the best marksman in the club—Quentin Brooks. He went first, firing at the darting blue rocks, and managed to strike 18 out of 25, standing at a distance of 25 yards from their release point.

Applause for this outstanding performance.

Then Annie stepped up and the crowd fell silent.

When the last blast faded, she'd hit 23 of 25.

Brooks bowed in concession to her superior skill while the no-longer-sedate crowd whistled and shouted their approval.

Lord Stanton, president of the East Sycamore Gun Club, stepped forward and presented her a souvenir of her visit—a gold medal larger than a five-shilling piece with some sort of engraving on it.

Doctor Llewllyn leaned over to Abberline under the applause, "That 20-gauge she's using is her favorite gun. Made special for her by Charles Lancaster."

"The famous gunsmith?"

"Correct. He saw she was using a shotgun that was too

heavy for her and didn't have the proper drop at the comb. She was undershooting her targets. He designed and fitted that one to her. Shorter barrel, too. Weighs only five pounds."

The applause finally died and the crowd broke up.

Abberline stepped down from the stands and stretched, feeling good. He hadn't thought of his job in more than an hour.

"Now to finish this day off with a good meal," the doctor said, pointing toward the clubhouse where the crowd was meandering.

"A meal? What was all that food on the table, if not a meal?" Abberline asked.

"Loosen your belt; you're in for a treat," Andrew Llewellyn grinned.

CHAPTER 6

September 28th, 1888

The door to Abberline's office stood open and Roger Clark, one of his inspectors, strode in. His wild red hair habitually defied comb or hair tonic, and this morning was thrusting up the usual rooster tails, side and crown. "Something you need to see," he said without preliminaries. He shoved an open letter and envelope across the desk. "It was sent over from the Central News Agency at Ludgate Circus. They treated it as a joke, but I'm not so sure."

Abberline looked at the envelope first. It was simply addressed, "The Boss, Central News Office, London City", and bore a postmark of Sept. 27, 1888.

The letter, written in red ink, read:

> *25 Sept. 1888*
>
> *Dear Boss*
>
> *I keep on hearing the police have caught me but they won't fix me just yet. I have laughed when they look so clever and talk about being on the right track. That joke about Leather Apron gave me real fits. I am down on whores and I shant quit ripping them till I do get buckled. Grand work the last job was. I gave the lady no time to squeal. How can they catch me now. I love my work and want to start again. You will soon hear of me with my funny little games.*

45

I saved some of the proper red stuff in a ginger beer bottle over the last job to write with but it went thick like glue and I can't use it. Red ink is fit enough I hope ha ha. The next job I can do I shall clip the lady's ears off and send to the police officers just for jolly wouldn't you. Keep this letter back till I do a bit more work, then give it out straight. My knife's so nice and sharp I want to get to work right away if I get a chance. Good luck.

> *Yours truly*
> *Jack the Ripper*
> *Dont mind me giving the trade name*

A second postscript in red crayon was written at a right angle to the rest:

> *Wasn't good enough to post this before I got all the red ink off my hands curse it. No luck yet. They say I'm a doctor now ha ha.*

Abberline looked up. "What do you make of this?"

"I'm not sure. It's just one of many crazy letters. First one I've seen that was signed that way."

"Giving himself the name, 'Jack the Ripper'. Has the head of CID seen this?"

"Yes. It was given to Sir Robert Anderson first."

"What was his impression?"

Clark shook his head. "It was a puzzle. He thought perhaps the salutation, 'Dear Boss', might indicate a Yankee connection, since that sounded like American slang to him."

"The rest of this wording more resembles a casually educated Englishman to me," Abberline said, stroking his sidewhiskers. So many practical jokers, so many cranks. How to distinguish them from the real threats? "Quiet for three weeks," he mused, turning the letter over in his hands. "Now Mister 'Jack the Ripper' wants to stir things up; he wants notoriety. You'll notice he didn't mail this to the police or Scotland Yard. He sent it to the Central News agency of the city of London. Besides whatever sexual thrills the killings produce, and the game of fox-and-hounds with police, he most of all wants publicity. He wants the world to read and shiver at his exploits. He's laughing at the law's attempts to catch him and he's warning us he's about to strike again." He got up and came around his desk. "I daresay the heads of the departments have conferred about this. But, to be safe, I'll walk this letter down the hall to Sir Charles. If this is from the killer, Mister Warren should want to increase his police coverage of Whitechapel. The constant, heavy presence of constables within whistle distance of each other on their beats might save a life. From what I've personally observed, surveillance has slipped a little, probably since nothing has happened for weeks."

"It's human nature to relax a little when things seem to be going well," Clark said.

"Probably what 'Jack' is counting on."

"Then why would he warn us?"

"Good question. I'd say he wants to make the game more dangerous—more thrilling."

"So you don't think this letter is a hoax?"

"Can't be certain, but I'm taking it seriously." He folded the letter and tucked it into his side jacket pocket. "Thanks for bringing it to my attention. I'll pass it along to Sir Charles."

"Would it help to compare the handwriting to the other letters we've received?"

"We have hundreds. It would take too long. Even if they found a match, what would it prove? That the same practical joker wrote more than one? It'd be worth the time and effort if it would tell us whether or not this writer is the real 'Ripper', as he calls himself."

He and Clark left the office together.

Abberline, frustrated from inactivity and lack of positive leads, decided to spend his own time this weekend prowling the streets of the East End. As a male, he had no fear of encountering the Ripper, but perhaps he could aid the constables.

He was glad to have something to call this lunatic besides the Slasher, the Phantom Killer, the Murderer, and other such names. The letter-writer had at least provided a more succinct cognomen, which law officers and newspapers could agree on. Somehow, it seemed to give the man an identity—Jack the Ripper—convenient and chilling at the same time. Visualize him however you might, the newspapers would jump on that name like a cat on a cricket.

Abberline had gone home from the office, exhausted from trying to figure out the problem and getting nowhere. He'd read all the reports of neighbors, witnesses, reconstructed the actions of the victims, viewed their backgrounds. All the suspects had been questioned, their lodgings searched, the acquaintances grilled. Each of the suspects had been in jail or a workhouse or a pub when a killing occurred, or were otherwise eliminated from suspicion because of circumstances.

When Abberline closed and locked his office door on Friday, he was convinced—as much as he'd ever been—that the police had done a very thorough job of investigation, but had not found any solid clues that might lead them to the killer.

He took the night off, ate a good supper, and read a few chapters of a light novel to prepare his mind for sleep. His rest that night was deep and undisturbed, even by the usual colorful dreams.

Saturday, he went to the police shooting range and spent two hours practicing with his handgun, refreshing his skills. He finally finished up, and signed out, leaving a record of his targets for the clerk to forward to the CID, updating his certification. He was not a natural marksman, but shot well enough, and often enough, to feel comfortable with his Adams revolver in case he should ever need it in a real emergency.

As he ate a light supper that evening at the Three Bells, he pondered the Jack the Ripper letter that was written in red ink in lieu of coagulated blood from a previous victim. That missive could have been the work of someone with a warped sense of humor, but Abberline had an uneasy feeling it was legitimate. When he'd first held it in his hands, he could almost feel an evil presence emanating from the page. He'd said nothing to Roger Clark who would've thought him daft. The longer Abberline was in detective work, the more he was bending toward the belief that those who claimed to be psychics might very well have powers beyond the ordinary senses. One or two who proclaimed such paranormal gifts had volunteered their services to the police, but their visions and predictions had proven false, so law enforcement officials had given up on them.

He shed his black ulster, draped it over the back of a chair, then stretched his legs and sat back with a tall, foamy glass. It would be a long night, so he needed to pace himself. The Three Bells didn't close until 3:00 a.m. and he meant to make it his headquarters between strolls around the streets. Even if nothing happened, he wanted to feel as if he were making an attempt to solve this case.

His Adams, cleaned and reloaded with fresh .450 cartridges, was snugged into a shoulder holster out of sight beneath his light jacket.

A bos'un's pipe shrilled. Abberline jerked out of a doze. Another shriek. Not a bos'un's pipe—a police whistle. Hands of the big clock above the bar pointed at 1:10. He leapt up, knocking over his chair. Three men and two women in the Three Bells stared at him as he dashed out, banging the door. The whistle? A block north. He sprinted in that direction, straight up the middle of the empty street, his shoes slapping on the wet cobblestones. He scanned both sidewalks as he ran, but noticed only two women and no men abroad at this hour.

The shrill whistle continued. Following the sound, he turned a corner. Half way up the block, someone held a lantern. He slowed, seeing other forms milling about, silhouetted by the gaslight at the far end of the block.

He pulled up, out of breath. "I'm Inspector Abberline of Scotland Yard. What's the trouble?"

"Constable Henry Lamb, Inspector," a man said at his elbow. "I was whistling for my partner up the street. Another murder, I'm afraid."

Abberline felt as if someone had kicked him in the stomach. "Where? How long ago? Who found her?"

"Over here. I've sent a man for the doctor, but I'm afraid there's nothing he can do."

Abberline followed the constable inside another fenced yard between two brick buildings. By the light of the policeman's lantern, Abberline looked upon a sight that had become all too familiar—a woman on her back with her legs drawn up. Blood running between the cobblestones had begun to coagulate. Her throat was a mass of blood, but, strangely, her face was placid, eyes closed. "My God, it's 'Long Liz' Stride! I just saw her in the Three Bells the other night. These women live on stolen time." His hand shook as he reached down and opened her fingers that still clutched something—a small packet of cachous, used to sweeten the breath. Her right hand was lying on her breast, smeared with blood. The long incision across her neck appeared to have been made from left to right—exactly as the others—indicating a right-handed attacker, whether she was facing him or away from him. There appeared to be no disembowelment.

Just then, another man pushed his way in alongside. "I'm Doctor Blackwell," he said, taking the lantern and crouching closer.

Abberline backed away. He'd seen all he wanted.

"A man driving his rig into the yard found her when his horse shied, sir," the constable said without being asked. "Empty warehouse on that side, but there's the International Working Men's Educational Club," he said, indicating a structure with lights on in two windows. "I'm familiar with it. A Socialist meeting place. Mostly Polish and Russian Jews. They held a debate there earlier this evening. People coming and going. The killer didn't have much time."

"I see," Abberline said, thinking that was why the victim

50

hadn't been further mutilated.

Anger and frustration. So near, yet so far. The Ripper was probably laughing at them right now—and from somewhere not too far away. Abberline wondered if the Ripper might have escaped by carriage—his own or an accomplice's. The police had already checked all the rental liveries within several square miles, and found no leads. All the cab drivers had also been questioned, to no avail. If afoot, he was likely still in the neighborhood. There were just too many streets and alleyways and courts in this congested section of the city to patrol them all. The entire police force of London would have to be assigned just to cover it.

He gritted his teeth.

He heard the clatter of shod hooves on cobblestones coming at a trot. A black Mariah passed a street lamp a block away. A few seconds later the driver reined to a halt and a constable stepped down from the box. "Is Chief Inspector Abberline here?

"Yes. What is it?"

"Come quickly, sir. There's been another murder a few blocks from here. Mitre Square."

"Let's go."

He followed the constable and they climbed in the back doors of the paddy wagon. The driver cracked his whip and they were off.

"Another prostitute?"

"Yes, sir. At least I believe she was."

"How did you know where I was?"

"When no one answered at your lodgings, we stopped at the Three Bells and asked."

"You made good time. When did this happen?"

"Barely a half-hour ago."

"Damn! We're only one jump behind him!" He slapped his thigh. "What else can you tell me about it?"

"Not much, sir. We set off to find you before we got all the details."

The rhythmic clopping was the only sound as the rubber-rimmed wheels rolled silently. The two men sat facing each other in the darkness.

The clopping slowed and the policeman on the box reined up. The two men stepped out the back door.

Abberline glanced about. "Another perfect setting," he muttered. Moving pools of lantern light illuminated the legs of several men. A low murmur of conversation.

"Who found her?" Abberline voiced his question to the knot of men.

"Edward Watkins, sir," a voice spoke up. The man stepped forward. "City Police Constable. I was making my circuit at fifteen-minute intervals. I went through the square at 1:30 and it was deserted. When I returned at 1:44 precisely, I flashed my light into all the corners as I always do. Found the body right over there. Come and see." Watkins led the way to a spot where a corner was formed by a brick building and a wooden fence. "This cobbled court is about 25 square yards and is enclosed by warehouses. Lots of traffic through here by day, but it's deserted at night. The street light doesn't penetrate back into these darker corners."

He flashed his bullseye lantern down at a rumpled pile of clothing that contained the mutilated body of a woman, lying on her back. Her throat had been cut and she was disemboweled. Blood on her clothes and the stones.

So the Ripper had done his grim work within fifteen minutes and gotten away without being seen.

A man was crouched by the body, a small black bag beside him.

"Police surgeon, F. Gordon Brown," the constable said in a low voice.

Abberline stepped back and bumped into someone.

"You got here quicker than I did," a familiar voice said.

"Andrew, don't you ever sleep?" Abberline countered, turning to greet his old friend.

"Will this grisly business never stop?" Doctor Llewellyn said as the two of them moved away to talk privately.

"Two in one night, within a mile, less than an hour of each

other," Abberline said. "And nobody saw or heard anything." He blew out a long breath. "Will you be doing the post mortem on this one?"

"No. A jurisdictional matter. Mitre Square is just within the boundaries of the city. She'll be taken to the City Mortuary at Golden Lane."

Policemen and spectators swarmed over the surrounding court and street, pools and beams of lantern light shining into corners, doorways and basement step-wells.

One of the constables approached. "Chief Inspector, I found something in the step well you should see." He held a bloody rag in the lantern light. "It appears to have been cut from the victim's apron."

"Likely used it to wipe his hands on as he was leaving," Abberline said. "I doubt he's anywhere around, but make sure to block off those stairs and question anyone up above."

"Yes, sir."

"Bag it for evidence, of course," he added, thinking it wouldn't bring them any closer to identifying the killer.

"Inspector Abberline! Over here!" Constable Watkins gestured and led the way through a brick archway. "Look at this." Watkins held up his light and Abberline saw a message chalked on the brick wall. He took out a notebook and a pencil and copied it down. *The Juwes are the men That will not be blamed for Nothing*

"What does that mean?" the doctor asked.

"I have no idea. Not even sure the killer wrote it."

"I'd testify it wasn't there before dark, or I would have seen it," Constable Watkins said. "This is a mostly Jewish neighborhood, sir, so that writing couldn't have been there long, or the Jews would have wiped it off."

"Yes."

Abberline put his notebook in his pocket and the three men exited the enclosure in time to see the body of the latest victim being lifted onto a hand barrow. "Careful, lads: Don't get blood on yourselves."

"Hold it. Hold it," an authoritative voice interrupted. The bearers of the body halted and set down the stretcher.

Abberline recognized the voice and the commanding presence of Sir Charles Warren who'd come on the scene. It was the first time he'd been called to one of these murders.

While someone held a light, Warren examined the woman. "Do you know her name?"

"Not yet, sir, but she'll be identified."

"Go ahead." The stretcher bearers started toward the hearse.

Warren looked around and asked a couple of questions, then spotted Abberline. "Ah, Chief Inspector, you're here. What have you discovered about this?"

"No more than you, sir. I just arrived myself from another attack only a few minutes walk from here."

"I was informed the Ripper had committed another of his signature mutilations."

"One of the policemen found this," Abberline continued, leading the Police Commisioner into the archway, and holding up the light by the brick wall.

"Rather cryptic message," Warren said. "Made by this Ripper fellow, I assume."

"We think it might be."

"Is he blaming the Jews, or is he saying the Jews will be blamed because this killing was done in their neighborhood?"

"It's anyone's guess, sir."

"Guess? We can't be guessing. We must apply proper detective work and find this man!" His voice rose slightly at the end. He frowned at the crudely-formed letters, biting at his lower lip beneath the heavy mustache. "This is not good."

Abberline looked at him, wondering what he was referring to.

"Get someone to scrub this off," Warren said.

"What? Sir, this is evidence. At least wait until a photographer can come and make an image of it."

"No. Write it down, if you haven't already, but I want it off that wall."

Abberline hesitated, looking sideways at Doctor Llewellyn. "I'm not sure I understand why you want it removed. Perhaps we could just drape a cover over it for now."

"I want it off—now!" Warren snapped. "I don't want a riot on my hands. If word gets into the newspapers about this inscription, people will be up in arms and the Jews will be blamed. The killer might be a Jew, or a Pole or a Russian or a mad Englishman. But, until we know, I want this wiped off. We will not have any race riots, in addition to everything else we have to deal with."

"I don't think that's a good idea, sir," Abberline persisted.

"I'm not asking your advice; I'm giving you an order." There was a note of near hysteria in his voice.

CHAPTER 7

"You have it, sir!" Abberline boomed, channeling his anger into his voice. "Constable Watkins, wet a rag in that rain barrel and rub the writing off the wall."

The constable cut a sharp glance toward Warren, but said, "Right away, sir."

Abberline groaned inwardly as his order was carried out. Sir Charles Warren stayed to ensure the cryptic message was completely gone before he lit a cigar and strolled away without another word.

"I'm not in the business of detection or law enforcement," Doctor Llewellyn remarked quietly. "But it seems only good sense to leave that message as possible evidence."

Abberline shrugged, trying to calm himself. "He had his reasons, whether I agree with them or not."

"Don't worry. You can tell me your real feelings," the doctor said.

"It's almost criminal," Abberline said. "That action will have serious consequences when word gets out." He turned away from the now-blank brick wall. "What I'm more concerned about is Jack the Ripper getting away again. We're so close, I can smell the brimstone," he grated between clenched teeth.

"No, what you smell is Warren's cigar," Doctor Llewellyn said.

Abberline took a deep breath and willed himself to be calm. "Are you going to assist at either of the autopsies?"

"I'll look in on both, but other doctors will do them. Come along if you like."

"Let's walk. I need some cool night air. Doubt if we could find a Hansom this time of night."

"You sure you want to walk these streets at two in the morning?"

"I have my friend—and he's ready," Abberline answered, patting his lapel that hid the shoulder holster.

"Let's go, then."

"I'll stop by the Three Bells before they close and collect my topcoat."

Forty minutes later, the two men were at the St. George's Mortuary. Before they entered, Abberline, out of long habit, filled his lungs with breathable, damp night air before he was forced to endure an atmosphere that reeked of formaldehyde, mold, urine and feces.

Police surgeon F. Gordon Brown and his assistants were waiting for a photographer who was setting up his bulky camera on its tripod and preparing to make an official record of the mortal remains of 'Long Liz' Stride. Four plates were exposed in the brilliant explosions of flash powder in the hand-held tray. The burnt powder drove out the odor of the place and was welcomed by Abberline, even though the smoke stung his nostrils.

"Now, doctor, if you'll remove one of her eyes..." the photographer said, moving his large camera closer to the table. "I want to backlight it for a closer shot."

"Do what?" Surgeon Brown asked, shooting a sharp glance at the burly, bearded photographer. "You want me to excise her eyeball? Why?"

"Commissioner Warren's orders."

"Where is Sir Charles?" Doctor Brown asked. "I need to get clarification of this."

The men in the room milled about for several seconds while someone was sent to the office to find him. Sir Charles came in and said, "Remove both eyes. Then a light will be placed behind them, and three photographs will be taken of the retinas. First the pupil will be illuminated, second, with the eyes illuminated as before, while the nerves are stimulated by an electric charge, and third, with the nerves stimulated, but with the eye not lit up."

"And what, exactly, is that supposed to show?" Doctor Brown was becoming irritated.

"Her retinas will retain the last image they saw, thus giving us a picture of her killer."

"Sir Charles, that's a popular misconception; there's no scientific basis for it."

"Have you ever seen it tried?" Warren snapped.

"Well…no."

"Then how do you know?"

Doctor Brown was silent under this chastising by his superior.

"We have a perfect opportunity to test it right now," Warren continued, apparently warming to his subject. "Her eyes were not damaged."

"All right," Doctor Brown conceded. "You want me to remove both eyes?"

"Yes."

"And place them where?"

"Position them upright on a table where I can get a strong light behind them."

This took some doing, but Liz Stride's eyeballs were finally in place. It was hoped by Charles Warren that these eyes, though they'd never see again, had retained at least their last image. The photographer and his assistant managed to make several exposures of them.

"There's no means here to set up an electrical stimulation," Abberline said under his breath to Llewellyn as they observed from several feet away. The doctor motioned for Abberline to follow him, and headed for the door.

When they were outside in the cool night air, Doctor Llewellyn said, "I assume the lack of an electric charge will be the reason given for that experiment not producing the desired result."

"Sir Charles is becoming desperate," Abberline said. "Did you know that old belief came from something in a Jules Verne novel?"

"Is that a fact?" the doctor said as they strolled away toward the City Mortuary. "Sounds good in theory, though, doesn't it?"

The two men fell silent. The dark street was deserted and Abberline almost preferred the sound of their voices to the silence as they passed along the deep shadows of doorways and alleys and courtyards. "Jack the Ripper," he said aloud. "I visualize him squatting beside Death, warming his hands at its cozy fire, chuckling madly at our game of hide and seek."

"I don't picture him at all," the doctor said. "To me, he's like a tornadic whirlwind that comes in the night, destroys and disappears. Who can capture a force like the wind? He's a disembodied spirit— the essence of evil."

"Oh, he most certainly has a body, and I won't be satisfied until it's locked up for life in the loony bin, or stretched on a gibbet."

"Sounds as if Jack the Ripper has become your very personal enemy."

"I'm trying to retain a professional attitude about this, but it's more difficult each time I see one of the women I've known in life disemboweled on the street."

Llewellyn nodded. "Prostitutes think no one in decent society cares what happens to them. They have a fatalistic attitude as well. I tried to warn one of them the other night about the dangers she faced."

"What'd she say?"

"Just shrugged. 'Oh, I know what you mean,' she said. 'I ain't afraid of him. It's the Ripper or the bridge with me. What's the odds?'"

"Yes, most self-styled Christians disdain them. Yet, Christ welcomed sinners and ate with them. That was one thing the Pharisees and the elders held against Him."

"Women of the streets are treated for injuries and diseases

at charity wards and workhouse infirmaries," the doctor said. "For most of them, unfortunately, it's not a very long step between first aid and last rites."

Dawn was graying the outlines of soot smudged buildings when, after a strenuous walk, they reached the City Mortuary.

The night watchman admitted them and they entered the post mortem room, quietly, edging around a small clump of men to get a view of the autopsy. Even to a medical layman, Abberline could see this woman had been slashed worse than Long Liz Stride.

"Have they identified her yet?" Doctor Llewellyn asked one of the workers standing beside him.

"Two of her friends said her name is Catherine Eddowes," the man replied.

"Well, at least she's now a person and not just a nameless corpse," the doctor replied.

The coroner looked up at the low voices in the room. "Ah, Doctor Llewellyn… Come closer, if you wish."

Doctor Llewellyn moved up to the table.

"Most extensive mutilations we've seen yet," Doctor George Bagster Phillips said. "Laid her open from pubic bone to throat. The tip of her nose was cut off and her eyelids slashed. There were also cuts to her cheeks. Of course, you were there where she was found so you saw the intestines had been removed, or at least cut out enough to be pulled up and placed across the shoulder. And about two feet of the intestines were cut off and placed between the body and the left arm. It appears to have been done by design, but I don't know why unless this was some sort of ritual." Doctor Phillips paused to allow the male stenographer to catch up with his dictated notes.

"Her death was caused by massive blood loss when the left carotid artery was severed, apparently by a left-to-right stroke that also cut through the larynx and down to the vertebrae. It appears the knife had at least a six-inch blade that was very sharp."

Standing behind the small group, Abberline listened to the

doctor's description of the injuries without attempting to see as they were pointed out. He had not developed a physician's immunity to such things. His cup was already running over—with blood. But he did force himself to take out his notebook and begin jotting down some of the details.

"The right ear lobe and auricle have been cut through..." Doctor Phillips continued. "Further cuts were made, opening the abdomen, extending across the thighs and across over the liver. The pancreas and spleen were also cut. The left kidney has been carefully removed. I should say that someone who knew the position of the kidney must have done it. The lining membrane over the uterus was sliced through and the womb cut through horizontally, leaving a stump of ¾ inch. The rest has been taken away. The removal of these organs would be of no use for any professional purpose."

"Doctor," one of the spectators interrupted, "would the killer be covered with blood when the carotid spewed out?"

"Probably not, because it appears she was strangled before her throat was slashed, so the heart had stopped, thus avoiding most of the gushing force. Besides, from the looks of the wounds, the killer was standing on her right side and probably behind her so he'd have avoided the blood when he reached around and slashed the left side carotid."

"I see."

"I don't think the killer is a doctor, but he does have considerable skill with a knife, and some anatomical knowledge to be able to do this kind of cutting within ten minutes, working by feel in a completely dark corner."

"Would a professional butcher have such knowledge?"

"It would be only speculation on my part, but I'd say 'yes'."

Abberline had had quite enough of this for one night. He'd read the report, or attend at least part of the inquest in hopes of picking up a clue he could use. He edged forward and touched Doctor Llewellyn on the arm, then silently signaled he was leaving.

Escaping from the fetid atmosphere, he sucked in the cool, damp outside air. It was balm to his lungs and his whole being, though

61

it was anything but pure, fouled as usual by sulfurous coal smoke, the smell of dank drains and uncollected horse dung, mingled with the nose-curling rotten-fish aroma wafting from the Thames.

A dull disc of sun was beginning to silver the foggy atmosphere.

Abberline heaved a heavy sigh as he walked along, hands in his coat pockets. It seemed he'd been doing a lot of sighing lately. Maybe it was time to take a little holiday from Jack the Ripper. He couldn't leave his job just now, so a mini-holiday would have to do. As an employee of Scotland Yard, he was entitled to use the Police Athletic Club, a privilege he hadn't taken advantage of in several years. His irregular hours provided him with an excuse for not exercising. Perhaps if he started to work out and get back into condition, he'd feel better, and not be so exhausted. The club was open in the evenings as well as during the day to accommodate mostly the younger policeman who walked their beats in round-the-clock shifts.

Where were all the pedestrians this morning? He'd seen few tradesmen, laborers, or landladies on their way to market, no shopkeepers opening their shutters.

Then a church bell from St. Bartholomew's chimed a few blocks away. He realized it was Sunday morning. He did an abrupt turn and started toward the sound. It wasn't just that he needed Divine help to solve this case of multiple, mutilating murder; he needed spiritual solace as well.

Although he attended St. Bartholomew's Anglican Church often, he was tired and felt that an aura of blood and death clung to his clothing. Arriving just as Mass was starting, he slipped inside and took up a spot in a back pew by himself.

After a few minutes of inactivity, his mind wandered and he had to fight to keep his eyes open during the liturgy and the sermon. He left at the last blessing, feeling much better for having been there.

Maybe Jack the Ripper would take a holiday on the Sabbath and give Death a respite, Abberline thought as he crawled into bed an hour later.

CHAPTER 8

Abberline was still in something of a fog Monday morning at his office. It wasn't until early afternoon that he became alert when red-headed Roger Clark rapped on his open door and quickly entered the room, obviously suppressing his excitement.

"The Central News Agency sent this over, sir. Apparently from the same correspondent." He handed a bloodstained postcard across the desk. The card read:

> *I wasn't coddling dear old Boss when I gave you the tip. You'll hear about saucy Jackys work tomorrow double event this time number one squealed a bit couldn't finish straight off, had not time to get ears for police thanks for keeping last letter back till I got to work again.*
> *Jack the Ripper*

Abberline turned the card over. "Postmarked in East London October 1st. That was yesterday—Sunday. The killings took place shortly after midnight on Saturday. This is very likely from the killer or he wouldn't have known about what he calls the 'double event' so soon. It hadn't even had time to reach the papers. If it's not from the Ripper, this hoaxer must have been in the neighborhood very late that night and heard people talking about it."

"Yes, sir."

64

"Has Commissioner Warren seen this yet?"

"Yes. In fact, he's ordered facsimiles of both this letter and the last one made and sent to the press and posted outside every police station in case someone recognizes the writing and comes forth with information."

"That's the first thing he's done for a while that I agree with," Abberline muttered. "However, it's going to generate a fresh flood of letters that we'll have to sort through. Make sure that original is safely guarded."

Clark left and Abberline picked up the top folder of several stacked on his desk. They were files put together on each victim, beginning with Polly Nichols, then one on Annie Chapman, and lastly, the most recent victims, Elizabeth Stride and Catherine Eddowes. The folders contained background information that was gleaned from friends and remains of scattered families, along with grisly photos taken at the morgue, revealing the mutilations, plus any and all notes about their comings and goings during the last hours of their lives. He'd been through these files before, so he only scanned the information quickly to see if anything caught his eye— anything at all he'd missed. Was there some pattern here? Other than their profession, did these women have anything in common that attracted the deadly attention of the Ripper?

He opened the file on Elizabeth Stride. One of her friends, who identified her at the mortuary, knew her as Annie Fitzgerald. This was a common occurrence; some women went by their maiden names and some by their former married names, some going by a first name, some by a middle name, nickname, or by a fictitious name altogether. According to testimony of witnesses at the inquest, she was regularly arrested for drunkenness, but whenever arrested for public intoxication, always denied she'd been drinking and stated that she was subject to fits.

A witness named Sven Olsson, the vestryman of the Swedish Church in Trinity Square, who'd known her for seventeen years, said her maiden name was Elizabeth Gustafsdotter. She was born on November 27th, 1843 in Torslanda Parish north of Gothenburg,

Sweden, the daughter of a farmer named Gustaf Ericsson and wife, Beata Carlsdotter. They lived on a large farm and the parents had another daughter and two sons. Elizabeth was confirmed in the church of Torslanda in 1859. In October of 1860, she left school and took out a certificate of altered residence from the parish and went to work away from her home in the parish of Carl Johan in Gothenburg. There she was employed as a domestic until 1864 for a workman named Lars Fredrik Olofsson, who had four children. She moved again and on February 2, 1862, took out a new certificate to the Cathedral Parish in Gothenburg, but her new home address was not known. She still listed her occupation as a domestic.

In March, 1865, she was registered as a prostitute by the Gothenburg police. The following month, she gave birth to a stillborn girl. The witness speculated she might have been forced into the streets to make a living because she would have very likely been let go from her job as a domestic for being pregnant. According to official records, she was living in October in a suburb of Gothenburg, is described as having blue eyes, brown hair, straight nose, oval face and slightly built body. In October and November, 1865 she had been seen in the special hospital, Kurhuset, for venereal diseases, but in the last four visits in November was stated to be healthy, and was told she no longer had to report to the police.

The following year, on February 7, 1866, she took out a new certificate of altered residence from the Cathedral Parish to the Swedish parish in London. The certificate indicated she could read reasonably well but had a poor understanding of the Bible and catechism. She was entered in the London Register on July 10, 1866. She was registered as an unmarried woman. Her first London employment was with a family in Hyde Park.

Although the record wasn't clear, she was thought to have married John T. Stride, a carpenter. She later claimed he'd drowned in a boat accident with two of their nine children. But a record of the passengers in the *Princess Alice* disaster showed no one by the name of Stride, and the only man and two children who drowned was an accountant and his two sons.

Abberline took a deep breath and turned the page. A twisting past, spiraling ever deeper into lies and deception. The official church records, at least, were devoid of any indication that she'd had a deprived, or abused childhood. On the contrary, the Christian church had kept close ties with her, or her with it. Apparently, it was the custom, when moving from one parish to another, to take out a church certificate to show change of residence and parish affiliation.

For the past three years she'd been living in Fashion Street with a waterside laborer named Michael Kidney. Now and then she'd earned some money by sewing and charring, but the couple often parted when she felt like going off on her own. The cause was invariably the same—her drinking. Kidney indicated he always knew she'd return to him in her own good time. It had happened often before. On the Tuesday prior to her death, she'd walked out on him and he didn't see her again until he identified her body at the mortuary. Depressed and heartbroken, he'd gone out and gotten drunk. Later that night, Kidney stumbled into a Leman Street police station and told detectives if he'd been a policeman and Elizabeth's murder had occurred on his beat, he'd have shot himself.

Abberline sat back and raked his fingers through his hair. Whatever the situation of their relationship or her past, Michael Kidney apparently really cared for her. Human love could exist anywhere under nearly any circumstances, and the longer he was a detective, the more he realized it. But caring family, church affiliation or no, a person still had free will and could deviate into another lifestyle altogether. Queen Victoria's grandson was a prime example. No one in the realm could have had more care and attention, or the material good things of life than Prince Eddy. Yet, he'd gone off on his own thrill-seeking adventures that were ultimately his downfall. In Eddy's situation, it might have been a case of having *too* much wealth and leisure, cosseted by too many tutors and family restrictions. The life of a member of the royal family was by no means easy.

Abberline leaned forward over the open folder and glanced down to the more pertinent testimony of those who'd seen Long

Liz in her last hours. A laborer, William Marshall, who worked in an indigo warehouse, said he'd seen Liz shortly before midnight on Saturday night some three doors from where he lived in Berner Street. He knew who she was by the clothing she was wearing—the same clothes he saw on her body later in the mortuary. She was talking to a man, but there was no street light near so Marshall couldn't see his face. The man he described as about five feet, six, and stout, and decently dressed. He had the appearance of a clerk, although he wore a round hat with a peak, something along the style of what a sailor would wear. Marshall testified the man wore a cutaway coat, appeared to have no whiskers, and carried nothing in his hands.

Marshall said he was standing in his doorway and didn't pay much attention to the couple, who were kissing. They stood there for a while before they walked away and Marshall said he heard the mild-voiced man say, "You would say anything but your prayers." Marshall added that the man appeared to be educated.

If the last statement was true, Abberline thought, it didn't square with the uneducated writing in the Ripper letters that he and Scotland Yard had accepted as genuine. So the man Marshall saw might not have been the killer.

He turned the page and his eyes alighted on the testimony of Police Constable William Smith. Perhaps, as a trained observer, this man would be more accurate and detailed. Constable Smith said he was on his beat on Berner Street that night and saw a man and woman talking together about 12:30 in the morning. Smith saw her face. Although he didn't know her personally, he recognized her later in the mortuary as being the same woman.

Smith said the man she was talking to was about five-foot, seven, wore a dark, deerstalker hat and a long, dark overcoat and dark trousers. Smith guessed his age at about twenty-eight and said he had a respectable appearance. In direct contradiction of Marshall's statement, Constable Smith indicated the man carried something wrapped in newspaper in his left hand. The package was about eighteen inches long and six to eight inches wide. But, then,

Marshall and Smith might have seen two different men. It wasn't impossible that Liz Stride had been with two men in the space of twenty minutes or so. Smith indicated the man was wearing a long coat, nearly down to his heels.

Abberline turned to the next sheet and read the testimony of the last witness. James Brown, a boxmaker, didn't have anything pertinent to add. He said he went out about 12:30 to get some supper from a chandler's shop in Berner Street. As he was crossing the street, he saw a man and woman talking, leaning up against a wall. When he heard the woman say, "Not tonight; some other night," Brown turned and looked at them. The man was leaning over her with his arm braced against the wall. He was wearing a dark coat, which reached almost down to his heels. Brown went on about his business, got his supper and carried it home. When he'd nearly finished eating, about a quarter of an hour later, he heard screams and shouts for the police.

Taking into account the discrepancies and faults of casual observations when recalled later, Abberline concluded that the men each of the witnesses described was probably the same person.

Abberline shut the folder, thinking that Long Liz Stride had not been mutilated to the extent the other victims had. True, she'd been strangled like the rest, and her throat brutally slashed, apparently after she was dead. But at least, she hadn't been disemboweled. "Small consolation, that," he muttered to himself. "The crazy bastard just didn't have time."

Abberline got up, stretched and walked around his office. He would have preferred to be somewhere else. The sunshine through the window told of a decent Fall day outside. But he forced himself to sit back down at his desk and take up another of the folders, this one on Annie Chapman.

One of "Dark Annie's" friends, Amelia Farmer, testified at the inquest that she'd gone to the mortuary to identify Annie. Amelia told the coroner that Annie had lived apart from her husband for four years. Her husband had been a coachman at Windsor. During that four years she'd resided in the lodging houses in Whitechapel and

Spitalfields.

"About two years ago, Annie and I lived in the same lodging house at 30 Dorset Street," Amelia Farmer said. "Annie was living with a man who made iron sieves. She was then calling herself Annie Siffey, or Sievey, because that was the name of his trade. At the same time she was receiving an allowance of ten shillings a week from her husband. About eighteen months before she was murdered, the allowance stopped. When Annie checked to find out why, she discovered her husband had died. She also found out what happened to their two children who'd been living with Chapman, her husband. Her son, who was born a cripple, had been sent off to a Cripples Home and her daughter to some institution in France.

"Annie was smart. She could do needlework and sometimes made a little money selling her crochet work. She also sold flowers. But then she'd get drunk, and went 'on the game' to get money."

Amelia went on to say she'd seen Annie two or three times in the week before she died. When they'd met on Monday, Annie had complained of feeling ill. At the time she had a black eye and a bruised chest, the result of a fight with Liza Cooper, another prostitute Annie had known for at least fifteen years.

"The fight came about over a piece of soap. Annie sometimes spent the weekend at the lodging house with a man known as 'The Pensioner'. He lived nearby in Osborne Street. Dark Annie borrowed a bar of soap for The Pensioner to wash with. She promised to return it, but she didn't. Liza asked her for it the next week. Annie tossed her a half-penny and told her to go buy some more. Later on, the two of 'em happened to meet in The Ringers public house. Liza was drunk and Dark Annie had been at the sauce too, and they started to have a few harsh words. They left the pub and kept at each other when they staggered into the doss house kitchen.

"Annie finally slapped Liza's face and yelled, "You best think yourself lucky I didn't do more!' Well, that started it, and the two of them went at it. Annie was short, but she was fairly stout. Even though she was forty-five years old, I'd a put m'money on her in a fight wi'Liza. But I'd a lost. Liza pounded and kicked her good.

When I saw Annie a few days later, she was still barely getting around and said she felt sick—I suppose from the beating. She looked bad. Then I saw her again the next day, on Tuesday, September 3rd. She still felt unwell, and said she was going to the casual ward for a day or two to rest. She hadn't had nothing but a cup of tea all day, so I gave her tupence for a cup of tea and told her not spend it on drink. Well, I didn't see her again until Friday when she said she was still poorly, and didn't feel like doing anything. But she said, 'It's no use my giving way. I must pull m'self together and go out and get some money, or I'll have no lodgings.' That was the last time I saw her alive."

An hour later, he closed the last file, stumped. The only thing they had in common was their occupation. Each had arrived at it from a different direction, although they were of the same general age—35 to 45 or so, had a similar pattern of broken marriages, followed by co-habitations with lovers or common-law husbands, estrangement from children, alcoholism, working menial jobs as charwomen, or making trinkets to sell on the street. These women knew each other, mainly because circumstances threw them together. Several were actually good friends and helped one another when more down and out than usual.

He picked up the Elizabeth Stride file again and read the testimony of a man named Israel Schwartz, a Hungarian Jew who lived in the neighborhood and had come to the Leman Street police station late on September 30th. On his way home late Saturday night, Schwartz was passing the gateway to Dutfield's Yard when he saw a man stop and speak to a woman in the gateway. The man tried to pull her into the street but turned her around and threw her down. She screamed three times, but not very loudly. Schwartz, not wanting to get involved, crossed to the opposite side of the street. There, he saw a man lighting his pipe. The man with the woman called out to the man across the street with the pipe, "Lipski". Schwartz walked away, but the second man followed him. Schwartz started running until he reached a railway arch where he turned around and found the other man had stopped chasing him. Schwartz told the police he thought the two men knew each other because of their exchange. He gave a description of each man.

Because the doctor determined 'Long Liz' was killed about fifteen minutes after Schwartz witnessed this exchange, the police thought the killer was not only a Jew, but had a Jewish accomplice named Lipski.

Abberline knew better. Being familiar with the area, he knew an Israel Lipski was hanged for the murder of a Jewish woman last year. Since then, his surname had been used as an insulting epithet to Jews in the East End.

He leaned back in his chair and kneaded the furrows out of his forehead. Even Queen Victoria's grandson, Prince Albert Victor Christian Edward, known as Prince Eddy, the Duke of Clarence, was suspected because he frequented whores and wild parties in the East End, and was known to have contracted syphilis. He even matched the general description of the killer. But when the police discovered he'd been in Scotland at the time of the murders, he was dropped as a suspect. For the sake of the elderly Queen and the Royal family, Abberline was relieved.

On the way home that evening, he stopped at the Police Athletic Club, signed in and began his long-delayed process of getting fit. Stretching, bending, walking, running, and much to his embarrassment, playing a game of tennis with a young constable who eased up to keep from totally humiliating him.

He finished up in the steam room.

"Janelle, that was good exercise. I need to lose a few pounds and get my wind back."

The young Canadian girl who checked in the members, monitored the equipment and managed the cloak room, smiled at him. "Inspector Abberline, I've not seen you in here before."

"It's been a long time," he admitted. "How did you know my name?"

"You signed the log. But, then, everyone knows who you are.

72

You're famous." She turned, retrieved his black ulster and handed it across the counter. "You'll be back, won't you?"

With a stunning smile like she had, how could he say 'No'?

"Yes. I'll try to make this a regular thing—if I don't die from overdoing it the first day."

The next morning he found out how badly he was out of condition when he could hardly get out of bed. Every muscle ached. He did some stretching exercises, but it only hurt worse. He knew from experience that it would get better with time. Meanwhile, he was in for a few days of pain.

As the first week of October wore on, Sir Charles Warren put every available policeman, even those from other divisions, to the task of investigation. Besides the distribution of Jack the Ripper's two letters to the newspapers, 80,000 leaflets were delivered to households and lodging houses in the area, appealing for anyone with information to come forth. The police detained at least eighty suspects and were watching the movements of a further 300, all follow-ups to information received. With permission of the landowners, house to house searches were made. More than 2,000 lodgers were examined during the first half of October. Sailors were checked by the Thames Police. All Asiatics were checked after an Indian correspondent to the *THE TIMES* wrote that mutilation to Eddowes' face seemed 'peculiarly Eastern'. Visiting Americans were checked, including three cowboys from Cody's Wild West Show. A total of 76 butchers and slaughtermen were questioned, as well as Greek gypsies.

Abberline managed to get in one more session at the Athletic Club before the weekend, but was too tired to do anything at all on Saturday or Sunday.

Abberline often went to Whitechapel and patrolled the streets himself until four or five in the morning. After one of these all-night sessions, he went home and slept a few hours, arriving back at his office in the early afternoon.

He had nearly stopped perusing the newspapers since they

were in full cry for the resignation of Sir Charles Warren. After what the papers were calling "The Double Event"—the two murders on the night of September 30th/October 1st—the papers indignantly called Charles Warren incompetent, and demanded his removal.

The ground in Regent's Park was white with frost at 7:00 in the morning of Monday, October 8th.

Abberline blew on his cold hands, wishing he were somewhere else, but Charles Warren had ordered him to be present, along with one constable, and three civilian officials from Scotland Yard. They were to witness the trials of two champion bloodhounds named Barnaby and Burcho. Their owner and handler, Mister Edwin Brough of Scarborough stood to one side, holding his dogs on leashes. A short, stocky men, he was dressed in tweeds and a soft cap, and sported a huge handlebar mustache .

Sir Charles explained what they were about to do.

"These are probably the best tracking dogs in all of England," the Commissioner declared. "Mister Brough has kindly agreed to let us test them to see if they might be useful in our search for The Ripper. First of all, I want Jim Carling to take off and run in any direction you wish. Just stay in the park." Warren pulled out his watch. "I'll give you a fifteen minute head start, then we'll turn the dogs loose and see if they can track you. Here, let them get your scent, Jim, so they'll be able to recognize it."

Carling, a man in his thirties, dressed in charcoal overcoat and leather gloves, came up and held out his hand for the dogs to sniff. The noses ran up and down his arm and his trouser leg.

"All right…Go!" Warren said.

Carling jogged away and was soon lost in the early morning mist that blanketed the lightly wooded park.

While the fifteen minutes dragged by, Abberline paced about, trying to stay warm and wished he had a good cup of tea.

"Turn the dogs, loose, Mister Brough," Warren said, snapping his watch closed.

Brough said something under his breath to the dogs, unsnapped their leashes and the ungainly looking animals trotted away in the direction of Carling who'd left an obvious track in the frosty grass. But the dogs kept their noses to the ground for a good distance before breaking into a run.

Rather than wait, the assembled men began walking in the direction the dogs had taken, though the animals were quickly lost to sight.

More than a mile farther on, they came upon Carling standing by a tree with the dogs wagging their tails around him.

"Excellent! Excellent!" Warren enthused, rubbing his hands as he came up. "They came straight to you."

"Right you are, sir," Mister Brough said, his face somber. "Bloodhounds are not put off by anything once they get the scent and I give them the order. Hares, birds, squirrels, other dogs, cats—nothing turns them aside."

"We'll try it one more time, and then have you come back tonight after dark and we'll give it a go to see if darkness makes any difference. And, if there is no frost tomorrow morning, we'll try it again."

The group dispersed, only to reassemble at ten that evening. The frost was gone and this time Warren, himself, took the part of the quarry. "I'll twist and turn and dodge and do whatever I can to throw them off the scent, just as the Ripper might do if he knew he were being tracked by dogs. Give me a fifteen minute head start."

For a middle aged man with a sedentary job, Charles Warren seemed very athletic, Abberline thought as he watched his boss run off into the dark, wearing a dark coat and pants.

The allotted quarter hour passed, and Brough released his dogs who put their noses to the ground, circled around a bit, then took off in a straight line like they were on rails.

More than a mile later, they found the bloodhounds who'd found Warren in spite of his having jumped across a small stream, walked up a sloping dead tree, backtracked and did whatever he could to throw off the trackers. To no avail. He was delighted with the result.

Twice more the experiment was conducted, both times successfully. Warren could not have been happier.

"Barnaby and Burgho are the best, sir," Mister Brough said. "If they can't track it, then it likely isn't there."

"We'll try it three more times in the early morning before any people are in the park," Warren said. "If they perform as well as they have so far, we'll have you keep them on standby in case there is another murder. Then the department will call on you to bring them quickly, Mister Brough. This killer won't get away again."

"I live a good ways away, Commissioner," Mister Brough said. "Wouldn't it be better if you was to take m'two dogs and put them up in a kennel someplace closer by in Whitechapel, so they'll be Johnny-on-the-spot, so to speak?"

"No, no. You take them home, Mister Brough. Just bring them back in the morning for one more trial. Then I'll be satisfied the police will use their services. I'm nearly convinced right now. In fact," he turned to Abberline, "I'm issuing an order tonight that nothing is to be touched at the scene of any future murders until we get these two dogs there and put them on the trail."

"Yessir. Do you think the dogs should be tested in Whitechapel first? This park is rather empty of other humans. Whitechapel is crowded with people who could be a distraction, plus the many conflicting smells and odors of humans, manure, dead fish, cooking. Might be a good idea to test them in that environment."

"Inspector Abberline, the tests here are sufficient. This park is frequented by many people whose scent probably lingers."

"Don't have a worry, inspector," Mister Brough said. "Once my dogs pick out a scent, it doesn't matter how many smells are mixed up with it. They can track it to the end."

"Your word is good enough for me," Abberline said. He was ready to go home.

"We'll try it once more tonight," Warren said, just getting warmed up to his task. "This time we'll have one of our constables who's very fleet of foot."

Abberline stood back to watch, wondering what the dogs would do if their quarry were to climb up a ladder to a pitched roof, or was picked up in a carriage. Controlled tests were fine as far as they went, but if The Ripper read in the paper that tracking dogs were to be used, he'd counter with some human ingenuity to elude them. Abberline was certain of that.

CHAPTER 9

Abberline was slumped at his desk several days later when Clark entered the office.

"Sir, this was delivered yesterday to George Lusk." He placed a small package, wrapped in brown paper, on the desk.

"Lusk? The man who heads the Mile End Vigilance Committee?"

"The same."

Abberline reached for the package. Lusk had no official status; he'd formed a vigilance committee on his own and set up shop in a pub, advertising a reward for any information or evidence submitted to him about the murders. At first uneasy about this vigilance committee, Abberline was now welcoming any help the police could get.

He opened the small box and recoiled slightly at its noisome, bloody contents. He looked up at Clark.

"Lusk took that to Doctor Llewellyn, sir, who had it examined at the City of London Hospital last night. It's the left kidney of a human."

Abberline felt a slight chill. "What else?"

"It's been preserved in spirits of wine."

"Not preserved well. It's half rotted."

"The package contained a letter also," Clark said, handing over a wrinkled sheet of paper.

Abberline took it without looking as he examined the

package wrapping for a postmark. Only two stamps and an illegible postmark, apparently smudged in transit.

He turned his attention to the letter. The script looked familiar, but he'd have to get their handwriting expert, Frank Evans, to compare this letter with the last one warning them of the last two murders. The letter read:

> *"From Hell*
> *Mr. Lusk*
> *I sent you half the Kidne I took from one*
> *women prasarved it for you tother piece I fried and*
> *ate it was very nice I may send you the bloody knif*
> *that took it out if you only wate a whil longer*
> *Signed Catch me when*
> *You can*
> *Mishter Lusk"*

"Doctor Llewellyn said the adult this kidney belonged to was in advanced stages of Bright's Disease," Clark said.

Abberline pulled out his scribbled notes he'd jotted down in the autopsy room. "Hmmm…Wonder how long the renal artery is?" he muttered.

"I'm sure I don't know, sir."

Abberline took a six-inch rule from his desk drawer. "This kidney has one inch still attached." He flipped over a page. "Catherine Eddowes still had two inches of the renal artery. If the entire artery is about three inches long, and her remaining right kidney shows evidence of Bright's disease, we can probably assume this is her kidney."

"The doctor at the hospital said it had been preserved in wine, sir. Aren't organs destined for dissection preserved in formaldehyde?"

"I believe you're right. If this was removed at the scene by the killer, he would have attempted to preserve it fairly soon by using whatever he could get—probably wine."

"Except for the fact that this note was inside the package, I'd dismiss it as another crank letter," Abberline said. "Strange spelling of some of these words," he added. "Most people tend to write as they speak. This man writes as if he has an Irish dialect."

"We can get Frank Evans in on this."

"Yes. Our resident handwriting expert can enlighten us as to whether this is an educated man trying to throw us off by trying to write like an ignorant person, or if he's really semi-literate, as this letter seems to indicate."

Frank Evans bent over his desk, magnifying glass in hand, the top of his bald head shining like polished mahogany in the yellow light from his desk lamp.

Finally, he laid the glass aside, propped his spectacles up onto his forehead and looked at Abberline and Clark. "The 'Dear Boss' letter signed 'Jack the Ripper' and the 'From Hell' letter with the kidney, were written by the same man. No doubt about it. See that little loop on the bottom of the capital 'R'? And notice the distinctive way he starts the 'J' in Jack with the tiny curl at the top." He turned the letters around so the two men could see. "More importantly, observe the way the writer makes heavy strokes at the beginning of his words and thins to a point at the ends in a downward, slashing motion. These are known as stabbing, or slashing strokes. This style indicates the writer has a nasty temper, and may like sharp knives."

"How appropriate," Clark murmured.

"What about this postcard that predicted the 'double event'?"

"Definitely not the same person, even though all of the writers are right handed."

"I brought along a random sampling of other letters the police have received. There are hundreds more. These have been dismissed as crank letters. See what you think." Abberline handed them over.

Evans spread them out on his desk, dropped his gold-rimmed spectacles onto the bridge of his nose and quickly scanned the missives. "One or two here are indicative of real personality or mental problems, but not nearly the same as those first two letters," he said. "For example, see this backward loop on the tail of the 'y' and the 'g'? That's what we call the 'felon's claw'. This was written by a person who has deep feelings of guilt. As an adult, this writer would set himself up for punishment by creating situations that result in familiar feelings of shame. Deep down, this person would believe he is worthless."

"It's amazing what you can glean from a few marks on a page," Abberline said.

"People have no idea how much of themselves they reveal when they put pen to paper," Evans replied.

"Are these just theories, or have they been proven?" Clark asked.

"Hundreds—no, thousands—of test cases have been studied through the years," Evans said, shoving his glasses up out of the way again. "It pretty much checks out. That's why a thorough study of handwriting can be a lifelong passion or profession." He pointed a pencil at the first two letters. "It's considerably more difficult to determine if a writer is trying to disguise his handwriting—for example, a natural right-hander writing with his left, or the other way 'round. Or, by slanting the letters at an odd angle. In my opinion, that was not done with the first two letters, and with the postcard here. The writers of those were writing their normal way. They are not well educated."

"Thanks, Frank, that's exactly what we needed to find out. Your expertise is invaluable."

"You're welcome."

Abberline started up the stairs to his office. "That helps confirm those letters are from the Ripper himself," he said to Clark.

"What about the postcard?"

"That doesn't fit the pattern. Could be we're dealing with more than one killer. Or, the original Ripper might have an accomplice."

"Then, again," Clark said, "the Ripper might be completely

illiterate and just dictated those letters to one of his semi-literate, nasty partners in crime."

"You're right. None of this really leads us any closer to the identity or capture of this maniac."

"If he's a maniac, he's a cunning maniac."

"As we both know from experience, they often are—clever, cunning, wily—while they're violent, anti-social misfits who become obsessed with something outside normal behavior."

"The human brain is probably going to be the next great study in medicine."

"Stop by my office, and bring those files on four of our primary suspects. We need to talk."

Ten minutes later the two inspectors were seated at each side of Abberline's desk with the office door closed.

"Look at these two photographs. This is Montague J. Druitt, and this is the Prince Eddy, Duke of Clarence," Abberline said, sliding two pictures, side by side.

"My God, they could be twins!"

"Exactly. Both have lean, handsome faces, each has short, dark hair, parted the same way, and each has a small mustache. The noses are nearly identical. They are near the same size and age as well. To make matters even worse, a face very much like both of these, has been identified by eyewitnesses as The Ripper."

"I thought we had eliminated Prince Eddy as a suspect because he was at the royal shooting lodge in Scotland at the time."

"That's true enough, thank God. Her Majesty has enough on her mind by having a wild grandson with bizarre habits and friends. Some time or other at one of these wild parties he frequents in the East End, he contracted syphilis from a prostitute and his brain is deteriorating. Even the queen of England has no power to reverse that. That would be depressing and embarrassing enough without having him also turn out to be Jack the Ripper. Although, I would think hanging would be preferable to dying of syphilis, as he's bound to do within a few short years.

"So, we can set him aside," Clark said, closing the folder and laying in on the corner of the table.

"Now, what about Montague John Druitt?"

"Well he's from a respectable family. His father and grandfather were both surgeons, and young Montague was smart enough to win a scholarship early on. Later, he had a year of medical training, but then dropped out of university and later went back to take a degree in law. However, he's not practicing, but has accepted a job teaching in a boys' boarding school in Blackheath. His father is dead, mother confined to a hospital for the insane for the past few months."

"Hmmm...I wonder if insanity runs in the family?" Abberline mused. "He has no previous criminal record. And his siblings have done well in the professions. Do we have anything that puts him near the scenes of the murders, other than these sightings and descriptions that could fit any number of men?"

Clark shuffled through the papers in the file. "Montague was playing cricket at Blackheath at 11:30 in the morning on the very same day that Annie Chapman was murdered only six miles away at 5:30 the same morning."

"Anything else?"

"He's an excellent athlete. Strong hands to strangle and fast enough to flee."

"That's stretching it."

"Yessir."

"But keep throwing possibilities out there. Everything must be considered. We'll keep Druitt as a suspect and put a constable on him to monitor his movements."

"What about Gull?" Clark asked, opening another file.

Abberline heaved a great sigh. "Yes, what about Surgeon, Sir William Withy Gull? He's been Physician Extraordinary to Queen Victoria since last year, and royal surgeon for several years since he successfully treated one of the children for typhoid in the early 1870s." He leafed through the few sheets in the file. "Not much to go on."

"A lot of rumors circulating about him, sir."

"Yes, I've heard a few of them. Let's see if we can untangle some of this. First of all, one of his duties as surgeon to the royal family is to look after the welfare of Prince Eddy, the Queen's grandson, who, by now has softening of the brain from syphilis. The story goes, that Gull follows Eddy to some of the wild parties in Cleveland Street. It's too late for Gull to save Prince Eddy from the consequences of his lustful follies, so the good doctor follows at a discreet distance to see if he can catch Eddy in the act of slashing. Supposedly, Eddy has a horrible fixation on revenge because one of the prostitutes infected him." Abberline shook his head. "I can't envision a seventy-year old surgeon who had a mild stroke last year, roaming the streets of Whitechapel in the middle of the night on such an errand, even though he has a private coach and driver to carry him about."

"Some are saying Gull, himself, is the killer," Clark said. "He *is* an ardent vivisectionist. And some of the cutting, such as the triangles carved on Catherine Eddowe's cheeks, the placing of the viscera on the shoulders and so forth, all points to some sort of ritual. Doctor Gull is a prominent Mason—a secret order much into ritual."

"Far-fetched supposition to connect the two," Abberline said.

"Then, let me play devil's advocate and propose this," Clark said. "You know of the medium named R.J. Lees? He's the man who's held séances for the queen when she was trying to contact her late husband. Lees is a spiritualist who claims to be a seer and has visions of future events. He claims to have had visions of two murders where the killer cut off the ears. And the ears were actually sliced off one of the women. He also said he saw a vision of the killer wearing a tan tweed topcoat to cover up the blood on his clothing. He even led the police to Surgeon Gull's house on Brook Street. When the police questioned his wife, she was horrified that Gull was a suspect. But then, the doctor, himself, showed up in the middle of the questioning and admitted, since his stroke, he'd had lapses of memory. When he'd come to himself after more than one of these blank periods, he found unexplained blood on his shirt."

Abberline absorbed all this in silence. "Circumstantial. We have no proof of anything. Now, if Doctor Gull had dropped his knife at the scene of the crime, for example, we might have reason to arrest him on suspicion. But, as it is, we could make a case for dozens of people who were seen in Whitechapel on the nights of the murders."

"Well, it turned out that Gull also has a tan tweed topcoat, just as Mr. Lees envisioned," Clark said.

"How many men in London probably have tan tweed topcoats?" Abberline asked. "We have to have something more tangible than that. We need some kind of hard evidence that connects one of the suspects directly to one or more of the victims. Besides, Doctor Gull is an old man weakened by a stroke. You think he'd have the strength to strangle these women?"

"Perhaps his coachmen, John Netley, did the choking and the surgeon finished with the knife."

"I suppose anything is possible."

"Have you considered the possibility that the killer could be a woman?" Clark asked. "Midwives are common in the district, and they go about with blood on their aprons and smocks when coming from assisting at a birth. No one pays them any mind because everyone is concentrating on finding a man."

"Unless the prostitute is a lesbian, do you think any midwife could get close enough to one of these prostitutes, allegedly for the purpose of sex, to kill her?"

"Just a thought."

Abberline pulled his watch from a vest pocket. "Well, we've frittered away most of an afternoon with those letters and these files. Let's give our minds a rest. It's time for us to be off out of here for the day."

Abberline walked to the Police Athletic Club on his way home. He would force himself to perform three workouts a week here, regardless of his other duties. He was determined to get fit once more.

Today he went through his routine slowly, stretching, jogging, not overdoing it. He'd learned a hard lesson after the first day when he'd been so sore. Now that the soreness had passed, he knew to go at it a bit easier.

Although reluctant to admit it, one of the things that made his workouts more endurable was the presence of the smiling blond woman who worked there, the one whose good looks and sunny ways brightened even the murkiest London day. He and the other members called her "Janelle".

"You'll need this tonight, inspector," she smiled as she handed over his ulster from behind the counter. "There'll be a nip in the air when the sun goes down."

"Thanks, Janelle," he said, dropping a coin into a jar that was placed on the countertop for tips. "Wish I'd started frequenting this club a long time ago. Maybe I wouldn't have aged so fast."

"You know, inspector, you'd look a lot younger if you shaved those side whiskers."

"Really?"

"Oh, yes. It would make your face look leaner, too. But leave the mustache—maybe just trim it a bit."

He rubbed a hand over the hedgerow of whiskers that stretched down from his temples, thickened across his cheeks and curved up to form the mustache. He glanced in a mirror fastened to the wall as he put on his hat. She was right. The facial hair had the shape and appearance of a harness. "You might have something there, Janelle. I'll give it a try." He shrugged into his black topcoat. "By the way, you know my name; what's yours?"

"Janelle Stafford."

"Have you worked here long?"

"Just over two years."

"I can't quite place your dialect. Where're you from?"

She chuckled. "I moved here from Victoria, British Columbia. But I was born in Devonshire. My parents migrated to western Canada when I was just a child. I was clerking in a store there, but decided to come back and see if I liked it better in my native country."

"Well, then, a belated welcome home." He wanted to ask her age, but thought better of it. Guessing, he'd put her anywhere from twenty-eight to thirty-three.

That night at home, he lathered up, stropped his straight razor on his belt and carefully removed the entire beard except the mustache, leaving the ends short and jutting out barely past the edges of his mouth. "Damn! She was right!" He turned from side to side, marveling at his reflection in the mirror. He was transformed. No longer did he see the stodgy, middle-aged Chief Inspector. Rather a leaner, thirty-five year old constable had emerged. "Now, to flatten my stomach, tone my muscles." He'd already lost down from 180 pounds to 175, and had a goal of 165, which should be about right for a man five-foot, nine. He grinned in spite of himself. "Janelle, m'girl, you not only have pretty eyes, you have observant eyes."

CHAPTER 10

After two murders were committed in the early morning hours of Sunday, October 1st, the month settled down, day following day with no further atrocities.

Abberline had nearly been lulled into complacency before the double event. This time, he vowed to remain alert, even as week toppled into quiet week in October.

Sir Robert Anderson, summoned back from extended sick leave in Switzerland, was given responsibility for the Ripper case by Sir Charles Warren. Anderson, out of touch with all the complexities of the ongoing investigation, proposed that a cordon be thrown around several square miles of Whitechapel. Instead of trying to protect the prostitutes, the police, he asserted, should arrest any woman found "on the prowl" after midnight. By conservative estimate, more than 1200 prostitutes worked the Whitechapel district, making this action obviously impractical. Sir Robert was heard grousing about these women getting real jobs. But, as Charles Warren pointed out, they had no saleable skills, and the two occupations normally open to them—charwomen, and hawkers of homemade trinkets—were already full to overflowing. Thus, most of them were thrown back on their only source of income for lodging and food—selling their bodies.

Armed with his loaded pistol, Abberline prowled the streets of Whitechapel alone three nights that first week, arriving late at the office next day after snatching a few hours of sleep. Then, dressed in his oldest clothes and a soft cap, he chose two nights each week at random to patrol in lonely vigilance. But he also managed to keep up his thrice-weekly visits to the athletic club. He was gradually rounding into shape. He cut back on the pints of bitters at the Three Bells, and his slight paunch began to disappear. He didn't know how much of his weight loss was due to change in diet, or lack of proper sleep, or physical exercise. Possibly a combination of all three. But it was working. He had more stamina, slept better at night and generally felt less stressed by his job. Several of his colleagues commented on his youthful appearance, without realizing he'd shaved his sidewhiskers and lost two inches off his waist. "I'm thriving on this case," he replied when turning away a compliment. "The Ripper has put me on my mettle."

That was at least partially true, he reflected. The rest of the truth lay with wanting to look good for Janelle Stafford. By some surreptitious inquiries, he'd confirmed she'd never been married. But she also made it a policy not to step out socially with any employee of the police department. And many of the vigorous young constables had asked her. Early on, Abberline deluded himself into thinking she favored him above all others. But his hopes were dashed when he heard the bantering that went on between her and each of the other men who worked out at the club. She loved them each and all, without exception or favor. She was a young, pretty version of their collective mother. From that point forward, when she complimented him on his youthful good looks, he took it as a well-meant compliment and nothing more. Each of the men was special to her, and she to them.

Friday, November 9th arrived. Abberline, having patrolled the streets of Whitechapel most of Wednesday night, retired early on Thursday night and arrived fresh at his office the next morning.

The first three hours of the day were taken up by routine work, reviewing files, reading reports of witnesses, poring over anonymous letters from the public, and trying to ignore the daily call in the newspapers for the resignation of Metro Police Commissioner, Sir Charles Warren, and newly appointed head of CID, Sir Robert Anderson.

At 11:00, Roger Clark stuck his head of unruly red hair around the office doorway. "Chief, are you going to take in the Lord Mayor's Day parade at noon?"

"Yes. I could do with a bit of a lift—band music and all that."

"Good. If you don't mind, I'll join you."

"Come back at half past and we'll go."

Abberline had hardly bent his head over his work once more when the thudding of running feet and cries in the hallway startled him. He stood up just as a uniformed constable burst into the room.

"Chief Inspector, come quick! There's been another murder in Whitechapel."

It was a sunny day, but Abberline, out of habit, grabbed his ulster from the coat rack and rushed out the door after the policeman. As they ran down to the curb and jumped into a waiting Hansom, Abberline tried to keep his mind a blank, and not anticipate what was waiting for him. During the several block ride, he and the Bobby didn't speak. To keep his mind on something else, Abberline thought of the nickname "Bobby" given to the uniformed constables on the beat. For some reason, he'd always hated that term, "Bobby", derived from the name of Sir Robert Peel, the man who'd organized the Metropolitan London Police force more than fifty years before. Probably meant as a compliment to the memory of Mister Peel, but it sounded undignified when applied to the dedicated men who enforced the law, day in and day out, armed only with truncheons, whistles and shiny blue helmets.

The Hansom drew up at Miller's Court, and the two men alighted. Abberline half expected to see a group clustered around a body on the ground, but the men and women were talking in low voices in twos and threes.

"Doctor Llewellyn."

"Inspector. I got here about fifteen minutes ago." He looked grim. "The worst yet."

"Who is it?"

"Mary Jane Kelly."

"Oh, no! The young, pretty Irish lass."

"She's not pretty any more."

"Where is she?" Abberline glanced around, noting the court had been cordoned off and constables on guard against anyone entering the street.

"Inside that first room at the head of the court."

"Let me see."

"The door's locked."

"Who has the key?"

"It's been lost. So says John McCarthy, the landlord."

"Then, how did you see her?"

"Come around here." The doctor took him by the elbow. Abberline nodded to the Bobby who opened the heavy rope to let them through.

"This window. That's how she was discovered an hour ago when McCarthy sent his assistant to collect the back rent." Doctor Llewellyn reached through the broken pane and drew aside the muslin curtain.

Abberline looked inside, and instantly wished he hadn't. The sudden impression that burned itself into his retina was the image of a body on the bed, so badly slashed and hacked as to be hardly recognizable. Blood on the sheets, the walls, the floor, flesh on the table. Pouring out through the broken window from the overheated room was a powerful stench of something burning.

He recoiled. "Let's force the door."

"The constable said he and the other police were given strict orders not to touch anything until bloodhounds could be brought to the scene."

"Oh, that's right. Warren's directive. Has anyone gone to fetch the dogs?"

"Don't know. A constable went to find Sir Charles an hour ago."

Abberline fidgeted, standing on one foot, then the other,

91

staring down the street, watching for Charles Warren, or for some conveyance that might be hauling the bloodhounds.

"Inspector, this is John McCarthy, the landlord," the doctor said.

"Fred Abberline." The men shook hands. "While we're waiting what can you tell me about this?"

"Not much, inspector. I rent this room to Mary Jane Kelly. She entertained clients in here now and again when she and her husband, Barnett, were separated—which was often. I don't get into the private lives of my tenants much, but she and Barnett got drunk a fortnight ago, started quarreling and one of them busted this window. And, since they'd lost the door key, they had to reach in through the broken window and turn the latch. I told her I'd fix the window when she paid me her back rent. She was in arrears to the tune of thirty-five shillings…"

"I thought the practice here was a night's rent for a night's lodging, paid in advance," Abberline interrupted. "Why did she owe three month's back rent?"

"Well, it's kind of a long story. Mary Kelly had been living with Barnett. He gave her the rent money, but she drank it up, more often than not. They had quarrels about her drinking, and whoring on the side. I didn't want to force things because Barnett had a job, of sorts, and Mary earned some from prostitution. But she's three months pregnant—I don't know by who—and was having the heaves in the morning, you know. She'd about run her string, as far as earning money from clients. The room's in Mary's name so I told her she could invite a female friend in to share the room with her, figuring Barnett would have to move out—which he did. This friend was whoring and earning, and Mary would let her use the room whenever she wanted. M'old lady and I figured we'd get the rent money with the two of them taking on clients at least part of the time."

Abberline nodded. Life was hard in the East End. "Who was this roommate?"

"Maria Harvey."

"Do you see her in this crowd now?"

McCarthy's gaze swept around. "No. I looked for her earlier, but I ain't seen her today."

"So, who found Mary?"

"I sent Tom Bowyer around this morning to collect the back rent, and he couldn't get no answer when he knocked, so he went around to the side here and pulled out the rags they'd stuffed into the hole in the glass. He got the shock of his life, and then come running to tell me. I sent 'im t'fetch the nearest constable. That's about it."

"Whoever was in there with her must've come out the door and reached back through the window to lock the place; that hole in the window's too small to climb out of."

"Reckon so," McCarthy said, scrubbing a hand over his unshaven chin.

"Did anyone see who she was with last night?" Abberline asked.

"I didn't, but there might be a few of her friends around here who could put y'wise to that. She ran with a few of these women who rent from me."

"Thanks. I'll want to question them soon."

Doctor Llewellyn took out his cigar case and offered a smoke to Abberline as the two men moved off a few yards.

"Thanks. I need one of these to get the stench out of my nostrils."

The doctor produced a match and the two men lit up. Abberline seldom smoked, especially now that he was working himself back into condition. But there were times, such as this, when a cigar was the only thing that could insulate his senses from such horrible things.

Curious onlookers came crowding up, and several of the neighbors thrust their heads out of upstairs windows to see what the fuss was about. Word apparently spread quickly about what the ground floor, number 13 Miller's Court contained.

And still they waited. Abberline finished his cigar, and ground out the stub under his shoe. He turned up his coat collar. The pale November sun had warmed the street as much as it would this day, but the air was still chill.

Abberline pulled out his watch. "It's nigh onto 1:30." Just as he snapped it shut, a Hansom drew up to the curb and a uniformed constable stepped out.

"Where's the commissioner?" Abberline snapped, irritated by the long delay. "Is he bringing the man with the bloodhounds?"

The constable had a strange look on his face. "Commissioner Warren won't be coming, sir. Nor will the dogs. Sir Charles resigned last night, and his resignation was accepted this morning by Home Secretary Matthews."

"*What?*"

"That's what I was just told at headquarters when I went asking for him." As if trying to emphasize the truth of his astounding statement, he added, "The story will be in the afternoon papers. Something about a clash of jurisdiction. But all that's beyond me, sir." He edged away.

"Let's go." Abberline reached through the broken window and turned the latch.

Doctor Llewellyn pushed the door and it knocked against a table by the bed. The doctor squeezed inside. Abberline turned and motioned for a photographer who'd been summoned and was waiting. "Get some good views of all this before anything is touched or disturbed," he told him as the big, bearded man hauled his bulky camera and tripod inside. The man never batted an eye. He acted as if he photographed scenes like this every day. He set up quickly, loaded his flash tray with powder and shot the room and the body from various angles, taking care not to touch anything or get blood on his equipment. Within a few minutes, he was done and departed to develop his plates in the lab.

Abberline shoved inside, leaving the door open to clear the smoke and let some of the heat out of the room from the remains of a fire. He was struck by how small the twelve-foot by twelve-foot room seemed. It was furnished only with a bed, two small tables and a chair.

Mary Jane was lying on her back, wearing a chemise or some type of linen undergarment. The body was near the edge of the bed nearest the door. The other side of the bed was touching the wall partition. The bedcovers had been thrown back.

"See how much blood is on the sheet and the floor over there?" Doctor Llewellyn pointed. "Her body was moved to this side of the bed after the carotid was cut. Almost sure that was the immediate cause of death."

Abberline, stunned by the sight, reluctantly looked as the doctor pointed out the obvious and the not so obvious.

"The throat's been cut right across with a knife, nearly severing the head from the body. The abdomen is partially ripped open and both breasts have been sliced off. The left arm is attached to the body only by skin. The nose has been cut off, the skin peeled from the forehead, the thighs stripped of most of their flesh. The nose, breasts and flesh from the legs have been placed on the bedside table. The abdomen has been slashed downward and the entrails and liver pulled out and liver placed between the feet. One of the hands of the victim has been pushed into her stomach."

During the doctor's recitation, done in a flat, unemotional voice, Abberline had completely forgotten to take out his pencil and notebook. It didn't really matter. He'd get it all later in the autopsy report if he needed it. "Her eyes haven't been damaged," he managed to say. "I wonder if the Ripper left them alone purposely to challenge the police to find his image in them."

"Not much telling what goes through that man's mind," Doctor Lllewellyn said. "Indoors here, he had shelter and he had time, so he let his blood lust have free rein. He could hardly have done a more thorough job."

While the doctor continued to examine the remains, Abberline turned his attention to the coal grate. "Looks like he tried to burn some clothes. Must have been a really hot fire," he said, raking at the embers with a poker and pulling out a tin kettle with the handle and spout melted off. He made a mental note to have the police sift the ashes. "Some women's clothing. Could have belonged to Maria Harvey, though" he added, noting Mary Jane's clothing neatly folded on the chair beside the bed. He wondered if the Ripper had tried to burn any of his own garments that might have been blood-stained.

"That's about all I can see here," the doctor said after fifteen minutes. "Have the body taken away to Shoreditch mortuary for a detailed post mortem and inquest."

As the two men exited, a one-horse carrier's cart turned into Dorset Street. Two men unloaded a scratched and dirty shell of a coffin that had obviously seen much use.

The crowd surged forward against the roped-off area. "Stay back, now folks," one constable said gently. "They'll be bringing her out."

Silence fell over the crowd. Caps were doffed and eyes glistened as the shell containing all that was left of Mary Jane Kelly was carried from the room, placed in the cart and driven away.

For some reason, Abberline felt drained as he watched the horse-drawn cart disappear around a corner. It was daytime and he'd had plenty of sleep, but his limbs felt heavy. He had a desire to go home, lie down and sleep for two days. Maybe he'd wake up and be relieved to discover this was all just a nightmare.

Doctor Llewellyn moved up beside him, slipping his coat back on against the November chill. "I know how you feel. This really took it out of me, too."

"Doc, she was a prostitute, and consorted with several men she called husbands. But, Lordy! She was only twenty-five, had auburn hair and sparkling blue eyes and the most charming Irish accent you ever heard. A laugh and sunny disposition you'd swear were bubbling up from innocence." He swept a hand at the throng around them. "See how they loved her."

Doctor Llewellyn shook his head. "And the further shame of it, she carried a three month old fetus who'll never see the light of day."

CHAPTER 11

The mutilation of Mary Jane Kelly was discovered at mid-morning and effectively put a stop to the Lord Mayor's Day celebration. When word reached the crowds lining the thoroughfare for the parade, nearly everyone left and drifted toward Miller's Court until the nearby streets were clogged with several thousand people. The celebration and the parade dwindled away and halted as the somber mood enveloped the multitude who'd turned out, anticipating a carefree holiday.

Even after Kelly's body was removed to the mortuary, it took the police more than an hour to completely clear the streets. Number 13 Miller's Court was roped off.

Doctor Llewellyn conducted the autopsy, assisted by Doctor Brown and Doctor Bagster Phillips. The extensive mutilations were recorded, and even the physicians, who by now were used to such things, remarked at the brutality of the attack. The knife that slashed her throat, for example, had cut so deep it nicked the neck vertebrae. After analyzing the remains, Doctor Llewellyn discovered that all the displaced organs and sliced flesh could be accounted for, with one exception—her heart was missing.

"Did that monster eat it?" Abberline asked Doctor Llewellyn two days later when the surgeon was giving a verbal summary of the post mortem findings.

"I shouldn't be surprised, given his statement in that letter that he'd eaten a portion of a victim's kidney," the doctor replied.

"He could have grilled it over that roaring fire he had going in the grate," Abberline said.

The doctor slowly shook his head. "A very twisted, angry man, indeed."

The two men were watching from a distance as Kelly's coffin was carried from St. Leonard's Mortuary in Shoreditch to make its way to St.Patrick's Catholic Cemetery at Leytonstone. Uniformed police had to clear a path through the mass of people jamming the street in front of St.Leonard's. The pallbearers finally reached the tall black hearse, opened the back doors and slid the coffin inside. Women in the crowd were openly weeping; men removed their hats.

"Well, it's not just the morbidly curious," Abberline remarked as the crowd slowly fell back to allow the passage for the team of black horses who were snorting and tossing their plumed heads at the crush around them.

The high wheeled, glass-sided hearse pulled away, the reins handled by a tall man in a black suit. Two mourning coaches, jammed to capacity, followed after.

"Who's the man up top with the driver?" Abberline asked.

"Henry Wilton, verger at St. Leonard's Mortuary. Since no one knows where her relatives are, he was determined she would have something better than just a pauper's funeral. He paid for all this himself."

The funeral cortege passed slowly along the street, trailed by several hundred on foot, many of whom would probably walk all the way to the cemetery.

"Fred, you think we'll have this many mourners at our own taking off?" Doctor Llewellyn asked quietly.

"Doubtful," Abberline answered.

"If all these people are testifying on her behalf, she'll probably walk right into heaven," the doctor continued, apparently in a reflective mood.

"I'm not going to speculate on that," Abberline said. "My job is to catch up with her killer who's still stalking the earth." He changed the subject. "Who's presiding at the inquest tomorrow?"

"Doctor Roderick MacDonald. He's a former police surgeon for K Division, and he's not happy about holding the inquest in Shoreditch at all, tying up the time of a coroner's jury. He contends the inquest should be held in Whitechapel since that's where the murder happened."

"I wish everyone would stop arguing about whose job it is and cooperate to help find this Ripper," Abberline said. "I'm getting sick of these everlasting squabbles. At the town hall?"

"Yes."

"Should be interesting. I imagine a lot of witnesses will testify."

"Since I led the autopsy, I'll be one of the first."

"Well I hope to get some useful leads from the testimony. The investigation has been thrown into a jumble since Sir Charles resigned. It's mostly a matter of jurisdiction. No one is quite sure who's giving orders to whom." He looked sideways at the doctor. "Did I tell you Queen Victoria sent a messenger to Scotland Yard late Friday?"

"No. What for?"

"Like everyone else, Her Majesty has a theory. Since most of the murders have occurred on weekends, she suggested the police check butchers who arrive on cattle boats that tie up weekends on the Thames before heading across the channel. Time enough for the killer to come ashore and do his dirty work, then disappear back to the boat."

"Probably as good a theory as any."

"I've seen those cattle boats," Abberline said. "They routinely travel from Ireland to Portugal, with stopovers here in London. *The City of Cork,* and *The City of Oporto* are two vessels that come to mind."

"I'm not convinced The Ripper has any special anatomical expertise, such as a butcher might have," the doctor said. "Any person of average intelligence can study an anatomy book with illustrations and gain a good idea where the various organs are located."

"Agreed. Besides, the police have questioned every butcher,

99

meat cutter and medical student they can find. If it's someone off a cattle boat, he must be very familiar with the Whitechapel district to be able to vanish so quickly and so completely. It's almost as if he knows where each constable is going to be and knows the routine of how they walk their beats. That's one reason we've put out so many plainclothes men to roam at random. I was one of them."

"Well, I was never very good at forming theories or solving puzzles," Doctor Llewellyn said. "Maybe that's why I'm not a good diagnostician."

"To each his own." He stopped walking. "I have to get back to the office. I'll see you at the inquest tomorrow."

"Until then." The doctor turned to flag down an approaching Hansom cab.

Doctor MacDonald began the inquest by establishing that the jurymen had all been taken to the mortuary over the weekend to view the body, completely covered, except for the face. One of the men described Kelly's face as looking like "one of those horrible anatomical specimens." Then they'd gone to 13 Miller's Court where they'd viewed the bloody room.

Abberline, settled into a wooden armchair at one side of the room, listened to the first witness, Joseph Barnett, the husband, as he told of last seeing Kelly at 7:30 p.m. on Thursday evening when she was talking to Maria Harvey. The court then elicited the information from him about her background. He said she told him she was born in Limerick, but had been taken to Wales as a young child where her father was employed in an ironworks. She claimed to have six brothers and sisters. At age sixteen she married a collier named Davis who was killed in an explosion two years later. Because of the long delay in receiving her compensation, she claimed she was driven to prostitution to survive. She moved to London when she was twenty, and then lived with a succession of four men at different times.

The next witness was a laundress, Sara Lewis, who went to

Miller's Court at 2:30 a.m. to visit a Mrs. Keyler who lived in the room opposite number 13.

Abberline wondered why she'd be visiting at that hour, but suspected she was a prostitute and didn't want to admit it in public. She described a man she saw standing outside the lodging house door—stout, tall and wearing a "wide-awake" hat. She was sitting in Mrs. Keyler's place, unable to sleep at 4:00 a.m. when she heard a woman scream, "Murder!" It seemed to come from just outside the door. Asked if she was frightened or if she woke up anyone else, she shrugged and said, "No, since there was only one scream."

A Mrs. Prater, another close neighbor, confirmed that she heard a scream around the same time.

Both women's statements coincided with medical evidence that Kelly had been killed between 4:00 and 4:30 a.m.

But Sara Lewis and Mrs. Prater were both contradicted by the next witness, a Mrs. Maxwell, wife of a lodging-house keeper at 14 Dorset St. She stated she saw Mary Kelly at 8:30 Friday morning at the corner of Miller's Court. She'd known Mary about four months. Mrs. Maxwell said she offered her a drink, but Mary declined stating the reason she was up so early was because she felt bad and had just upchucked a glass of beer. This coincided with morning sickness. Mrs. Maxwell sympathized with her and they had a brief conversation. Half an hour later, Mrs. Maxwell saw Mary outside the Britannia pub talking to a man in a plaid coat. She said Mary was wearing a velvet bodice, dark skirt, maroon shawl, and no hat.

There was considerable murmuring among the spectators when she finished her testimony since Mrs. Maxwell's statements had put Mary alive less than two hours before her body was discovered.

Abberline discounted this testimony in his own mind as a probable case of mistaken identity. He accepted the medical estimate for time of death at not later than 4:30 a.m.

Doctor Llewellyn was then called, and began to give the autopsy findings, but the coroner cut him short. "No need to go into all the grisly details, doctor," Doctor MacDonald said. "By making all that information public, we might be interfering with the police investigation. Please confine your testimony to the direct cause of death."

Llewellyn shifted uneasily in his chair, but said, "Mary Jane Kelly was found dead from the mortal effects of the severance of the right carotid artery."

The coroner rose from his chair. "I do not propose to hear any more evidence today. A verdict as to the cause of death can be drawn from what we've already heard. It is not the jury's duty to uncover the murderer." He turned to the jury. "If you've heard enough to render a verdict, you may do so now. If not, we can adjourn and reconvene in a week or fortnight and hear any additional evidence you wish."

There was a stir in the gallery.

The jurymen whispered among themselves. Then the foreman stood. "We have heard enough. We, the jury, find that the deceased met her death at the hands of a person, or persons, unknown."

Abberline was stunned. The inquest had lasted only half a day. He sought out Doctor Llewellyn as the crowd filed out of the town hall building.

"Never saw anything like it," the doctor said. "A truncated inquest when there was still much to be heard and made part of the official, public record. Politics reigns."

The next day, Abberline was in his office, scanning the newspapers that were still crowing over the resignation of Sir Charles Warren, whom they all considered a hindrance to a proper investigation. True or not, he was gone, and the Metro police were in the hands of an interim supervisor.

Roger Clark came to the office door. "Inspector, another witness on the Kelly murder has come forward, and the police want you to hear what he has to say. He's downstairs in the hearing room."

"Send him up here. More congenial surroundings."

"Right away."

Five minutes later, a man came in, holding a soft cap in his hands. He doffed a well-worn cape, hanging both on the coat hooks.

"I'm Inspector Abberline." He shook the man's calloused hand. "Have a chair, Mister…?"

"George Hutchinson, sir."

"No need to be formal here," Abberline said, closing the office door. Instead of going behind his desk, he pulled up a straight chair a few feet away.

Hutchinson looked to be about forty, somewhat taller than average with a lean, weathered face and slender, wiry build. He'd dressed in well-worn tweed jacket, but had on his scuffed work boots.

"I need to tell you some things that might help with the Mary Jane Kelly murder." He glanced furtively over his shoulder as if to be sure they were alone in the room.

"Why didn't you come forward at the inquest yesterday?"

"I planned to, but it ended too quickly before I could get off work."

Abberline wondered how many others should have testified, but never got the chance.

Hutchinson leaned forward in his chair, clasping and unclasping his hands between his knees.

Abberline sat back. "Relax and just tell me what you know. Take your time. We have all day."

"I'm a simple man, sir. A laborer who works hard for a living."

Abberline nodded.

"I was in Romford on Thursday and I walked back to London. It's a good, long way, and I got back to Whitechapel about two the next morning on Friday. I saw Mary Kelly at Flower and Dean St. I've known her about three years, and give her money occasionally when she needs it. She asked me for sixpence, but I told her I'd spent all my money going down to Romford. She said she had to find some money and she started off toward Thrawl St. A man coming the opposite direction tapped her on the shoulder and said something. They both laughed and Mary said, 'All right'. The man responded, 'You will be all right for what I have told you'."

"Those were his exact words?" Abberline had taken a pad from his desk and was busy scratching notes on it.

"Yes, sir. I'd stake my reputation on it. Then he put his right hand around her shoulders. He had a small parcel with a strap around it in his left hand."

"You're very observant."

"Yessir. It's my nature. Besides, Mary Kelly was a friend, and I wanted to see who she was going off with. I stood against the lamp by the Queen's Head pub and watched them. As they passed me, the man hung his head so his hat covered his eyes. I stooped down to get a look at his face, and he looked very stern at me. I followed them and they turned into Dorset Street. They stood on the corner for a few minutes and the man said something I couldn't hear. Then Mary said, 'All right my dear. Come along and you'll be comfortable.' He put a hand on her shoulder and kissed her. She said she'd lost her handkerchief. He pulled out a red one and gave it to her. Then they both went into Miller's Court. I followed but couldn't see them. I waited around for about forty-five minutes to see if they'd come back out, but they didn't."

"Can you describe him in a little more detail?"

"Well, he was around thirty-five years old, medium pale complexion, about five foot, six inches tall, dark eyes, dark hair, a small mustache turned up at the ends. He was otherwise clean shaven. No side whiskers. He wore a long, dark coat, collar and cuffs trimmed with astrakhan. Underneath, he had a dark jacket, light waistcoat, white collar and dark necktie fastened with a horseshoe pin. Dark felt hat turned down in the middle. He wore button boots under spats with light buttons. He had a thick gold watch chain with a big seal and a red stone hanging from it. He walked softly, and gave sort of a respectable Jewish appearance."

"Would you know this man if you saw him again?"

"Yessir. I'll never forget the look of those eyes when I

saw 'em close up. In fact, I thought I saw him again on Sunday in Petticoat Lane, but I didn't get a good look and couldn't be sure."

"I see." Abberline was scribbling notes as fast as he could write. "Would you be willing to give this description to the press? You don't have to give your name.

"Yessir." Hutchinson nodded, emphatically. "I was a bit nervous about coming forward earlier because I thought somebody might've seen me hanging about Miller's Court and identify me as the killer. Mary Jane was a friend of mine, and if there's anything at all I can do to help you catch her killer, I'll do it."

"Excellent. Wait right her a minute and I'll have my clerk take down your description in shorthand. He'll read it back to you to make sure he's got it right before it's given to the press."

Abberline rose from his chair. "If you're serious about helping us find this killer, there's one more thing I'll ask of you."

"Anything."

"I want to send you with two constables to patrol the streets of the East End tonight to see if you can spot this man. Will you do it?"

"Gladly."

"Do you have any family obligations to tend to?"

"I'm a bachelor, sir."

"Good. I'll call the clerk."

Abberline left the two alone in his office and walked outside in the cold November air. He was more excited than he'd been in weeks. Here was a witness who apparently was very observant with an eye for details. George Hutchinson had to have seen The Ripper. His description even coincided, in most details, with the general descriptions of some other witnesses. This killer did not stand out in a crowd. He dressed and looked and acted like many other men, and passed unnoticed by the Whitechapel residents. Many outsiders passed through the district. Hutchinson, who lived in Whitechapel, had not recognized this man, so he was possibly a stranger or a visitor. But now that Hutchinson had gotten a good look at The Ripper, hopefully he could spot him again. Since the killer was apparently still confident he could avoid detection, he'd likely be on the streets, bold as ever. Abberline prayed The Ripper had satisfied his gruesome blood lust long enough for the police to get their hands on him before he struck again. They were as close now as they'd ever been.

CHAPTER 12

But it was not to be. George Hutchinson, with two constables, patrolled the streets of the East End until three in the morning, part of the next day, and then until four the following morning. Nothing was seen of their quarry.

Abberline's early enthusiasm gradually waned as the days wore on, and the man Hutchinson had seen was seen no more. Hutchinson's detailed description had been given wide circulation by the press. But there were no more sightings by several thousand pairs of eyes who were on the lookout. The publicity did produce several hundred letters and verbal reports from the public. He was seen in Dorset St. or in the Britannia pub, or in Buck's Row, or on Old Montague St. The police followed up on all these reports that had even the faintest chance of being true. But if The Ripper had ever been at any of these places, he was long gone. On several occasions, a nearby constable on the beat was called within minutes of sightings, but the suspect was always missing by the time he arrived.

After two weeks, Abberline was on the point of despair. The police and Scotland Yard had done everything humanly possible to apprehend this criminal, but it seemed as if Divine intervention was going to be required for success.

One afternoon Roger Clark entered his office carrying two folders. "Chief, what are we going to do with these two suspects? Nothing new has been added to these two files for several weeks."

On the tab of the top file were the block letters, SICKERT, WALTER. Abberline flipped it open. "I don't recall that we have much, if anything, on this man."

"He's a prominent English artist who has a studio in the East End and associates with a number of prostitutes in the district. A morally bankrupt profligate, if I may say so."

"That's not a crime. What else?"

"He's in his thirties, unmarried, paints rather strange, grotesque paintings depicting the lower classes, and is able to sell enough of his paintings to make a living. In fact, he has something of a reputation as an artist, although his paintings make my skin crawl."

"Don't be a snob, Roger. We don't all have the same artistic tastes."

"He has plenty of opportunity and always seems to be close by when a murder is committed. I'm told he actually admires the brutality and audacity of The Ripper and even wears a red scarf around his neck as a symbol of blood when he's creating some of his gruesome scenes on canvas."

"Has he shown any antipathy toward prostitutes?"

"Not to my knowledge. Although, since he's intimate with at least two of them, he's threatened those two when they go whoring with other men."

"Not unlike a few of those prostitutes' husbands," Abberline said.

"Perhaps jealousy to the point of murder?" Clark wondered.

"Possible, human nature being what it is." Abberline said. "So he has been heard to threaten these women?"

"Yes, on several occasions."

"The Ripper would not likely do that. We're dealing with a man who would not go around growling or threatening. He'd more than likely be quiet, then explode when ready and the savagery would burst forth. More like a wolf with 'dumb rabies'."

"He likes to dress up and play the part of an eccentric, arrogant artist, has even performed on the stage, but not very successfully. He is a consumer of women. Has fathered more than one illegitimate child."

"So, what we know for sure is that he is a painter with what's known as an artistic temperament who uses women, but doesn't necessarily harm them, physically. He's a braggart, a hedonist, a poseur, possibly a frustrated actor who likes to constantly play a role in his daily life and wear a red scarf to scandalize his friends and ape Jack the Ripper," Abberline summed up, leafing through the file. "Again, no hard evidence, but a man who will bear watching."

"What about this man?" Clark said, sliding the other folder over. The name was KLOSOWSKI, SEVERIN A.

"I've gone through this file thoroughly Abberline said. "Born in Poland, trained as a physician, abandoned a wife and migrated to London two years ago and located in Whitechapel earlier this year. Failed to make it as a doctor, so he's been working as a barber's assistant, doing things like lancing boils and other minor surgical procedures. He's been living and working in the district during the murders and worked in a shop under a public house at George Yard, very near the Martha Tabrum murder site." Abberline reeled off the information in a monotone, knowing it almost by heart. He looked up. "He had opportunity and he has the surgical skill. But did he do it? At this point, he's shown no signs of violence and we have nothing to connect him with any of the murders."

"Damn!" Clark exploded, slumping back into his chair. "When are we going to get a break in this case? The public thinks we're not doing our job."

"Besides writing letters giving us their favorite theories, the public is not doing the exhausting legwork necessary to pick up clues or evidence," Abberline said, with resignation. "Keep these two files active for now." He closed the folder and slid both of them across the desk.

"Yessir." Clark picked up the files and left the office.

A sense of frustration, bordering on despair, was creeping over Abberline, but he dared not communicate that feeling to his subordinate. He'd never been involved in anything that had taxed his energy and resourcefulness like this case. He could think of nothing the police or Scotland Yard had not done. Policemen disguised as women were sent out on patrol. Abberline smiled ruefully at the mental picture. The Ripper would have to be very drunk, indeed, to mistake one of those big-boned constables for a female prostitute. The Ripper struck where and when he chose, with no discernible pattern, except that most of the murders were on weekends, and between midnight and six in the morning. Apparently, he was driven by some perverted desire or compulsion that had nothing to do with logic. In the meantime, every prostitute lived on stolen time.

From all available evidence, The Ripper was soft-spoken, genteel, wore the clothes of a somewhat down-on-his-luck gentleman. A cunning individual, he was nothing at all like Stevenson's Doctor Jekyll and Mister Hyde who drank a formula to change from mild physician to blood-lusting maniac. And he most certainly did not fit the description given to Abberline by Beth Hampton, a prostitute at the Three Bells. She'd been introduced to absinthe by some of her friends, and later told Abberline she'd had a vision of The Ripper. "He was coming for me like a hound from hell, in a halo of green marsh gas, wearing his bones and blood vessels on the outside like some ghastly coat. His hair was all asquirm with maggots and his eyes were ablaze like live coals. I could hear that foot-long knife blade whistling through the air when he slashed it back and forth."

She went on to say she'd never touch absinthe again.

Abberline checked his watch, then heaved himself out of his chair and headed for the door. Another frustrating day. He'd walk home, stopping on the way at the Whitechapel Workhouse where a man fitting The Ripper's description had been seen the previous night. A slim lead was better than none.

By the time he reached the workhouse, the sun was only a red disc in the west, unable to penetrate the murky atmosphere of London's exhalations. A line of destitute men and women stretched from the door down the block and around the corner, queued up early, each hoping to obtain one of a limited number of available cots for a night's shelter in return for some kind of maintenance work in the morning.

Abberline went to the head of the line, where a man sat behind a wire-grated window. "Wait your turn, mate. We ain't open yet." The man said without looking up.

"Inspector Abberline of Scotland Yard," he said, flipping back his ulster to reveal the badge pinned to the back side of his lapel. "I'd like a word with the manager."

The clerk got up, moved to one side and unlocked a door. "He's on the second floor. End of the hall."

Abberline climbed the creaking wooden stairs and found a middle-aged man in a cubbyhole office. He introduced himself.

"What's the problem, Inspector? We run a respectable place here."

"We got a report that a man fitting The Ripper's description stayed here last night."

"Is that a fact? Well, I wouldn't know nothing about that. What'd he look like, exactly?"

Abberline described the man as being about five foot, six, slender, clean shaven except for a small mustache, dark hair, dark coat, possibly a gold watch chain.

"Lordy, that description would fit arf the men who come 'ere, except for the gold watch chain. He'd uv had that stolen from him as soon as it got dark. If my clerk had seen that chain he wouldn't a let the man inside. We search 'em for weapons and such, ya know. Have to be destitute to stay here—no money atall."

"Yes, you're right." Abberline, who'd been standing in the doorway of the tiny office, stepped around the corner and looked into the long room. "Your casual ward?"

"That's it."

The long room contained two opposing rows of bunks. Each was actually a set of square iron frames bolted to the floor. A three-foot wide strip of canvas was rolled up on one frame. To form the cot, this strip was unrolled and fastened to its opposite square frame six feet away. A blanket was supplied to each sleeper.

It reminded Abberline of his time in the navy, except the

sailors' bunks had been suspended from the overhead. He'd enlisted at age seventeen and served four years in one of Her Majesty's smaller war ships, helping police the British Empire. He glanced out one of the shadeless windows at the glowing red ball that seemed to be resting on the rooftops. He'd seen just such a hazy sun sinking into the sea off the Azores. With little stretch of his imagination, he could still hear the bos'un's pipe shrilling across more than a quarter-century of time. It sounded very similar to the police whistles he heard nearly every day now.

"Anything wrong, inspector?"

The manager was standing at his shoulder.

"No. No. That's all, thanks. If you happen to see a man meeting the description I gave you, please send someone 'round to Scotland Yard right away."

"I'll do that, sir."

He clumped down the stairs and out to the street. Now to the athletic club for a hard, fast workout, home for a light supper and then bed.

Tomorrow he'd get up and do the same thing all over again.

"Ad in," Abberline called to his opponent across the net, a young, lithe constable. The man bent at the waist, standing flat-footed to receive the service, looking as tired as Abberline felt. The cement floor was painted a light green to make it easier on the eyes and to simulate a grass court. Several gas lights in sconces around the walls gave a semblance of daylight.

It had been a grueling, best of three set, two-hour match. Abberline stepped back from the baseline, wiping sweat from his brow and stalling to catch his breath. His opponent was twenty years his junior and Abberline had never defeated him. But now he was within one point of winning the match.

He toed the baseline, tossed the tennis ball into the air over his head and brought the racket through, slamming the ball into the opposite court. The constable caught it back-handed at the last instant and flicked it back. Then they had it back and forth—baseline shots, corner shots, short drops, forehand cross-court shots, dashing front to back and side to side in desperate lunges to make impossible returns of almost sure winners.

Finally, Abberline saw a slight opening and slammed a forehand with all his strength down the line and past the constable for the deciding point. It was all he could do to walk to the net without staggering to shake his opponent's hand.

"Great match, inspector!"

"Tom, admit it now," Abberline gasped, "you were sand-bagging, weren't you? You let me win."

"On my honor, I was playing as hard as I could, inspector." The two men walked toward the dressing room. "You've come a long way since we started hitting a few balls in here weeks ago."

Abberline nodded. "Hope I've made some progress. I was in pitiful condition."

"If I didn't know better, I'd say you were picturing me as Jack the Ripper tonight," the constable laughed. "I could see that hate in your eyes."

"I have to take out my frustrations on somebody, Tom. Thanks for understanding."

"I think that's one reason this club is here."

"Janelle, you're still working?" Abberline asked, twenty minutes later as he was checking out. "I thought the night shift would be on by now."

She smiled, handing over his topcoat. "I'll be leaving in ten minutes. But I'm applying to change my shift so I'll work from midnight until eight in the morning."

"Why?"

"Less work. Fewer men come in during those hours to work out. I'm studying up to go back to school, and I have time to read during those quiet hours." She hesitated, looking serious. "I haven't read or heard about any progress in the Ripper case the past week or so."

"There hasn't been any." He lowered his voice. "I get the uneasy feeling he's about due to strike again, although he doesn't follow any kind of time table." He shrugged into his coat. "The days are getting short. You don't have to walk far in the dark, do you?"

"Oh, no. I room with an aunt, and she has her own conveyance. Picks me up right at the door in a closed carriage."

"Good."

"You know, Inspector, I suppose everyone is giving you advice about how to catch The Ripper, so I won't add to that. I'm sure you know your business better than anyone else. I will say, though, that maybe a woman would be able to bait him, bring him out of hiding. These prostitutes know how to lure men. It's an instinctive thing with women."

"We've thought of that, and have put out some constables dressed as women. Didn't work."

"I don't mean that. I mean a real woman."

"We tried one woman with no luck. Couldn't try it again because the Home Secretary found out and banned that. Said if we got an innocent plant killed, it would be worse than if another prostitute died. In my opinion, he feared the bad publicity more than he wanted to catch The Ripper."

"If you don't mind my being so frank, some women give off a scent, a musk, if you will, like some of the wild animals I've studied in Canada. If you can find the right woman, it could work."

"And if you don't mind *my* being just as frank," Abberline replied, "this killer is not after sex. He's not normal."

She blushed slightly. "It could be these killings give him some kind of sexual pleasure. I still think it could work if you find the right woman. Don't be chasing him; make him come to you."

Abberline thought for a moment. "Let me give that some serious thought, Janelle. I think you might be onto something."

"No charge for the advice, inspector." She gave him her sunniest smile as he waved and went out the door.

PART TWO

CHAPTER 13

Inspector Abberline huddled down in his coat collar as a November wind gusted through the grandstand, blowing around old newspapers, showbills, and greasy fish and chips wrappings. The crowd wasn't bad for a chilly late autumn afternoon, but there were clusters of empty seats in the corners and near the top of the stands.

He watched a dozen whooping, mounted Indians pursue a Concord stagecoach around the huge grounds, stirring up dust. Men atop and inside the Deadwood Stage were firing blanks at the Indians. It was all mildly amusing to him; he was sure it was only a shadow of the real American West.

He reflected that the seasons were changing quickly; Summer was only a memory and Fall was fading. He'd waited almost too long. Within a fortnight, the Congress of Rough Riders of the World, also known as Buffalo Bill Cody's Wild West Show, would strike its tents, pack its tons of gear, load up hundreds of horses, mules and buffalo, and entrain for Southampton where the huge entourage would board a ship for the United States after a six-month run in London.

By the time the performance ended to a roar of applause, Abberline was standing by the gate where the performers retreated behind hanging canvas walls.

He stopped one of the stock handlers who was unsaddling a pinto. "Where might I find Colonel Cody?"

"Wal, if he ain't gone off somewheres, he's likely in his tent up to the end of the row there." He pointed.

"Thank you." Abberline started that way, dodging the costumed performers, both white and red, feeling conspicuous in his gray felt hat and black overcoat.

He saw the famous man from a distance. Cody sat with both tent flaps open and tied back. He was at a folding table reading a newspaper, cigar clamped in his teeth. He still wore his leather leggings, tall riding boots and bright yellow shirt. His gauntlets lay on the table. Flowing, straw-colored hair swept out from under the white hat and over his collar.

Abberline hesitated. How to approach this personage? He coughed. "Colonel Willaim Cody?" he said aloud. "Buffalo Bill Cody?"

Cody lowered the paper and took the cigar from his mouth.

"Might I have a word with you?"

"If this is about the rent on the grounds, my business manager, Nate Salsbury handles all that."

"It's not about the rent."

Cody stood up and stepped outside, looking taller in his white hat than the reported six, one. "Then I'm all ears. What can I do for you?"

"I'm Chief Inspector Frederick Abberline of Scotland Yard. Is there some place private we can talk?"

"Sure. Right in here." He ushered Abberline inside. "Have a seat. Hope I'm not in any trouble for anything. Did I do something at the Duchess's party the other night I shouldn't have? I'll admit to having one more drink than I shoulda. But you know how it is when a man gets to socializing." He smiled under the sweeping mustache. This handsome American was like a gust of wind off the Great Plains.

"No. It's nothing like that."

"Have a cigar?"

"No, thanks."

Cody sat back on the opposite side of the table and crossed

his legs, waiting.

Abberline scarcely knew how to begin, although he'd been rehearsing it in his mind since morning. "I daresay you've read about these murders committed by a killer who calls himself, Jack the Ripper."

"Read about it? Our show has had to compete with him for coverage in the papers for weeks," Cody said, not quite as jovial.

"Then you also know he's still at large."

Cody nodded. "I was just reading in the paper here where the Home Secretary, Henry Matthews, says you're on the verge of making an arrest in the case."

"As a showman yourself, you know everything is not always as it's portrayed."

"That means you have no idea who he is or where he is."

"That's about the size of it, as you Americans might say."

"I assume you're here for a reason."

This man wasted no time coming to the point. "Frankly, Scotland Yard and the Metro Police have nearly exhausted all our ideas about how to capture this lunatic. He follows no pattern, has no obvious motives, such as robbery, since these women he so cruelly mutilates are among the poorest of the poor. He has it in for prostitutes, but we don't know why. Some personal vendetta of his own. Because this man is obviously deranged or operates on some sort of perverse logic we can't understand, we need to use some unconventional means to capture him—some method we don't normally use on other violent criminals." Abberline paused, arranging his thoughts.

"Go on."

Abberline took a deep breath. "You have in your show a woman—Annie Oakley—who's probably the world's greatest marksman."

"She's a wonder, a true phenomenon."

Abberline plunged ahead. "No sense beating about the bush. We want her to be a lure to trap the Ripper."

Cody didn't reply or change expression. He looked across

at Abberline with his luminous eyes that stared out from so many posters and photographs, had seen so much of the world, both good and bad.

The drawn out silence became unnerving for Abberline who said, "We would take all precautions to ensure her safety, of course."

"No one can ensure that, if she's to be used as bait for a trap," Cody said.

"She can handle any weapon with speed and accuracy."

"That's like putting your head in an angry lion's mouth," Cody observed, "and hoping you have the speed and reflexes to yank it out again before he chomps down."

Before Abberline could reply, Cody went on. "You're either going to scare off the Ripper with too much protection. Or he'll kill her and then your men will kill him. In either case, it's a bad idea." Cody sat silent, staring directly at him with a gaze that had probably cowed many a poker adversary.

"No telling how many of these women might be killed," Abberline said. "He's worse than a rabid dog. He must be stopped. And, frankly, we've about run out of options."

"You know I can't let my star attraction take a chance like that," he said in a voice as matter of fact as if he were negotiating to buy a horse. "I pay her a handsome salary, but not to be used as a lure for a madman."

"I realize how you feel, but..."

"My answer is *no*. Do you realize what would happen to this show if she were killed? We'd lose at least half our revenue. You've seen the way she draws crowds since we've been in London. She's become the darling of the Brits. Certainly there are other marksmen, some of them men, who are almost as good. But she has a girlish charm, an athleticism, combined with a giant talent that just draws people to her—both men and women. People are fascinated by a petite, pretty woman who can beat a man in a man's sport. 'Little Missie' has it all." He paused and relighted his cigar that had gone out. "However preposterous this request to turn her into a manhunter, I won't give you a final answer until I call her in here and let you ask her yourself."

Abberline felt a resurgence of hope. Perhaps he could persuade her in person.

"Just a minute." Cody got up and threw back the tent flap. "Frank!" he called. "Frank Butler! Go get Annie and you two come in here a minute." He came back inside and opened two wooden folding chairs.

In a few minutes, Annie Oakley entered the tent followed by her manager/husband, Frank Butler. She was even prettier up close than Abberline had remembered when she performed at the shooting club—lustrous, dark hair and eyes, straight nose, regular features. She was still dressed in her white blouse, dark, short jacket, pleated skirt and leggings she'd performed in a bit earlier.

The couple sat down and looked curiously at Cody and Abberline.

Cody made the introductions. "Inspector Abberline has something to say, and I want you to hear it directly from him. Go ahead, inspector…"

Abberline repeated his proposal. He finished with the statement, "You'll be adequately compensated for your services whether the venture is successful or not. If we succeed in capturing this man, you'll have the gratitude of the British people. I can't think of a nobler way to end your tour here."

"I can't do it," Annie said, without hesitation. "I'm a performer, not an undercover policewoman."

Frank Butler also shook his head. "I can't let my wife expose herself to such danger. If the police have had no success dealing with this maniac, how do you expect Annie, with no law enforcement experience, to do it?"

"You would be paid…" Abberline began.

"Compensation is not the issue. I would do it for nothing, if I decided to do it. I don't need the money. The fact that I can handle rifles, pistols and shotguns and can hit most everything I have a mind to, doesn't mean that I could ever shoot a human being."

"We must think of this person, not as a human being, but as

a wild beast, possibly a rabid wolf or a crocodile that, once having tasted human flesh, cannot be weaned from it. No…that's not a good metaphor. Animals kill to eat. This monster kills for no reason that we can discern. Yet he kills and mutilates. I'm sure, if you read the papers, you've seen all the gory details."

"Mister…er…*Inspector* Abberline, we would surely like to help out the police, but this is something that is just too far-fetched for us to consider," Butler said.

Annie cast her husband a sharp glance. "Frank, I can speak for myself. I know you're my manager, but this is something personal."

Butler sat back in his chair and crossed his legs, opting out of the conversation.

Abberline felt uneasy in the presence of this domestic disagreement. Apparently, what he'd heard about Annie Oakley being a very self-willed woman was true.

"Inspector, this is a very unusual request," Annie continued. "I've had many strange offers in my life, including proposals of marriage from strangers, challenges to shooting matches, including a challenge to shoot a cigarette out of the mouth of Kaiser Wilhelm of Germany. But this tops them all. This is also the most dangerous, if what I've read about Jack the Ripper can be believed."

"Believe it," Abberline said. "The details of his killings have not been exaggerated in the tabloids."

Cody was looking from one to the other of them. "Just so you'll know, Little Missie, I told the inspector 'no' when he first came in here. First off, because of the danger to you, and lastly, because it would hurt the show if something—God forbid—should happen to you in the attempt to capture this madman. You can be darned sure it wasn't the money I was thinking about."

Neither Annie nor Frank responded to this. Abberline wondered if he'd gotten himself into the middle of a personality or money clash between these two parties. "Well," he said, rising, "it was worth a try. And I thank all of you for taking the time to listen to me." He bowed to Annie and nodded to Cody and Frank Butler. "Good day to you."

He ducked out the tent door and replaced his hat.

"Oh, inspector," came Annie's voice behind him. "How would I contact you if I should have any more questions about this?"

He felt a slight ripple of hope as he fingered a business card from the pocket of his waistcoat. "Scotland Yard, ma'am. There's the address."

CHAPTER 14

It was former Commissioner Sir Charles Warren who'd first hinted that Abberline might try some unconventional approach to trapping The Ripper.

Only now had this hint taken root when Abberline, in desperation, appealed to Annie Oakley for help. But his appeal was in vain, so it was best forgotten, he thought as he rode alone in a Hansom cab back to his office. She'd turned him down, flat, and been backed up in her decision by husband, Frank Butler, and her boss, Colonel William F. Cody—probably the two most influential people in her life at present. Yet, Annie'd shown she was her own person. She'd left the door ajar, and a glimmer of hope shone through the crack.

What if everything he planned came to pass? Just the thought caused a sinking feeling in his stomach. If Annie accepted, and was able to lure the Ripper to attack her, but then was severely wounded or killed, it would haunt him the rest of his life. He could be fired and even jailed for such a foolhardy attempt. Only if the effort were successful would he be praised. It was all or nothing.

He let his imagination run, uninhibited, through the details of the setup: She'd have to work alone. Yet, how could he or the police possibly be close enough to protect her at the critical moment? A long-range rifleman? Too many things could interfere—darkness, surprise, speed of the attacker, obstacles such as fences or buildings. He began to perspire even in the open cab. It was one thing to risk his own life, but to risk the life of an international well-loved celebrity, quite another. He'd be lynched. He began to wish he hadn't even mentioned such a crazy scheme. But he couldn't let go of it. Perhaps she could wear a rigid, protective collar, as some letter writers had suggested. It would be concealed by a scarf. That way, if The Ripper got his hands around her throat, he couldn't choke her, and the collar would also protect her from a slashing knife.

But it didn't really matter; she'd said "No", so that was that. Perhaps he'd been influenced by Janelle Stafford and her talk of female musk attracting males. What foolishness! Dealing with Jack the Ripper was like a child playing with explosives.

Annie Oakley was flustered. But as she bowed and skipped out of the arena the next afternoon, nobody would have known it, least of all her husband/manager, Frank Butler. The bloom in her cheeks could have been from the chill and from exertion.

But Frank was more perceptive than she knew. "Did you miss those targets on purpose?" he asked.

"Don't I always have to miss now and then?" she asked, brightly. "If I'm too perfect, the crowd will begin to think our act is rigged. It was only one clay pigeon and one coin."

He nodded, apparently satisfied, then gestured toward the continuing applause. "Curtain call."

She skipped out, waved to the crowd, curtsied and skipped back behind the hanging tarp. Audiences liked to think of her as a little girl excelling in a grown man's sport. Her diminutive size and characteristic skip accentuated this juvenile, playful image. She started toward her tent, Frank following with three of the long guns.

Matt Vickers, casually known as her "gun boy", or just "her boy", finished loading the traps, the shotgun shells, the boxes of glass balls, stacks of clay pigeons, a small sack of silver dollars, a mirror, apples, playing cards, three holstered revolvers and other small items into a padded wheel barrow and trundled it after Butler.

Annie stepped into her floored tent, knowing her misses

had *not* been intentional, but the gasp and the groan when the clay pigeon fell, unbroken, let her know the audience was with her, that they realized she was still human, after all. She hesitated to admit to Frank the misses were accidental, the result of lack of concentration. She was distracted, but had to let on everything was fine.

She was a performer—an actress. She felt a bit guilty about keeping anything from her husband. After all, she and Frank had only each other. And it had been so since she'd bested him in a shooting match on Thanksgiving Day at Cincinnati in 1875 when she was only fifteen years old. The Irish born Butler, ten years her senior, was surprised, then fascinated, charmed and in love. They were married only a few months later, then went on the road, she acting as an assistant to Frank and his male shooting partner as they performed one-night stands and week-long exhibitions all over the Midwest and East. Then, one fateful night, Frank's partner fell ill and Annie stepped in to replace him for the evening. She never left. The partner recovered, but left the show, while Annie and Frank became a team, moving on with their own husband-and-wife shooting exhibition. Later, when they joined Buffalo Bill's Wild West Show, Annie became the star and Frank willingly gave up his own career to act as her manager and assistant.

The spacious two-room tent was their home on tour, and she'd grown very fond of it. She pulled off her embroidered jacket.

Frank laid the guns on a long table. "Nate Salsbury and Doc Carver want me to play poker for a couple hours before supper," Frank said. "I'll load the rest of those shotgun shells this evening."

"Fine," Annie replied. "I need to do some sewing. Might even take a nap. Didn't sleep too well last night."

"Not riding your bicycle today?" he asked.

"Too chilly."

He came up and slipped his arms around her. They'd long since come to consider Matt Vickers as their surrogate son and thought nothing of showing affection to each other in front of him.

"You look a bit tired," Frank said.

"It's been a long season."

"Maybe we should take next year off," he suggested.

"And do what?"

"Whatever we want, and at our own pace. We could always hook up with a small show, or go on the road by ourselves for part of the summer."

"I don't know…"

"I'd miss all our friends in this show too, but variety *is* the spice of life." He looked around at Matt who was laying out the weapons ready for cleaning.

"We need to meet with Cody again," Frank said.

"I'm not up to it right now," Annie replied, sliding gently out of his arms.

"On the ship going home, then, after the tour is over in a week or two. We need to find out if he's going to keep Lillian Smith."

Frank could have said anything without bringing up that chubby teenager's name, Annie thought. Aloud, she said, "Okay. Then we'll ask about our contract and decide about next year."

"See you at supper, then." He smiled and ducked out of the tent.

Annie dug out her needlework and sat down in her favorite rocking chair. Winter was coming on and she couldn't sit outside in the sunshine as she'd grown accustomed to doing all summer. Their Franklin stove was warming the tent and she let down the flaps to retain some of the heat.

"Matt, when you finish cleaning those guns, you're free for the rest of the day."

"Yes, ma'am."

While her hands were busy, the routine stitches left her mind free to wander. The source of her distraction was Inspector Abberline's visit yesterday. She couldn't get his strange request out of her mind. She'd turned him down. Scotland Yard must be desperate to make such a preposterous offer. She should have forgotten the whole thing ten minutes after Abberline left. But here she was, twenty-four hours later, still turning it over in her mind, to the point where she'd misfired on one easy shot and one fairly difficult shot, but one she'd made hundreds of times. That must not continue.

What if…just supposing…she agreed to try to lure this Jack the Ripper character into a trap? The very idea gave her a chill and she shrugged her shoulders and settled more comfortably into the rocker. This man who'd been slashing women—he had to be stopped. So what if he selected only prostitutes for his attacks? They were helpless women who took money for a pleasurable act that was normally related to love. She wasn't shocked by prostitution, as many self-righteous women proclaimed to be. It was simply something that existed and she ignored it. When she thought of it at all, she felt pity for these vulnerable women. If she knew any of their backgrounds, she'd lay odds the majority of them had not set out to make it their chosen profession. From what she'd read, many of them had been forced into it by circumstances. In any case, she was in no position to judge.

There was a time when she was vulnerable as well—when she was not the world famous sharpshooter, Annie Oakley. It was a time when she was just dirt poor Phoebe Ann Moses, living in the backwoods of Ohio. She didn't willingly resurrect those memories. Maybe the pain of her childhood would soften with time, but now the scenes flashed, unbidden, into her mind's eye again.

In 1855, her father, Jacob Moses, had pioneered a homestead in Darke County, Ohio, eighteen miles north of the county seat of Greenville. With the timber he cleared from the plot of land, he built a log house. It was there she was born in August, 1860, and christened Phoebe Ann, but her older siblings dropped the Phoebe and called her 'Ann'. It was subsistence living, but the family did reasonably well for the first few years of Annie's childhood. They butchered a cow and tanned the hide to make shoes. They smoked hams, pickled beans and stored apples for the winter. Annie remembered her fascination with nature and the surrounding woods where she loved to walk, pick flowers, wild cherries and blackberries.

That early, hard-working but idyllic life ended abruptly when her father set out on a blustery day in early 1866 to drove a buckboard full of wheat and corn to a mill, fourteen miles away. A blizzard roared in and he finally arrived home after midnight, nearly frozen. Even though a doctor was called, he sickened and died.

Not long after that, Annie's oldest sister, Mary Jane, died of consumption, and mother, Susan, had to sell the milk cow to pay for the funeral. Susan attempted to support her family as a midwife, but could not. She sold the hardscrabble farm and rented a small wooden house. But Susan finally had to let her youngest, Hulda, four years Annie's junior, go live with another family named Bartholomew. When Annie was ten, Susan sent her to live at the county poor farm, a place known as the Infirmary, near Greenville. Before she could really get settled into her new environment, a man came to the Infirmary looking for a girl to serve as a companion for his wife and new baby.

It was this period of her life that still haunted her. The farmer and his wife used Annie as a slave. She got up at four in the morning, fixed breakfast, milked the cows, washed dishes, skimmed milk, fed the calves and pigs, pumped water for the cattle, fed the chickens, rocked the baby to sleep, weeded the garden, picked wild blackberries and got dinner. Even though she received a letter from her mother to come home, the family wouldn't let her go. She was held a virtual prisoner. They beat her for the slightest thing, raising welts on her back. One night the farmer's wife threw her outside into the snow and barred the door because Annie fell asleep over some darning.

Even now, Annie shivered at the terrible memory. The farmer finally came home from town and let her back in, or she would've frozen to death. And things got worse from there. Some abuse her mind had completely blocked out and only hazy impressions remained. From that time to this, she'd never uttered their name in public. They were fixed in her memory as "The Wolves".

Shortly before her twelfth birthday, she finally escaped by running away and returning to the poor farm. There she lived with the new superintendent, Samuel Edington, and his wife, Nancy, who was a friend of her mother's. They treated her as a daughter and she began attending school with the Edington children. After a time, the Edingtons paid Annie to work as a seamstress and she sewed dresses and quilts for the Infirmary inmates. She learned to embroider and stitched fancy cuffs and collars to brighten up the orphans' dark dresses. Seeing that she was very responsible, the family put her in charge of the Infirmary dairy. She milked the cows and made butter of the cream, all the while saving what money she could.

She finally returned home when she was fifteen. All the time she'd been away, she hadn't touched a gun. But she recalled being a natural marksman after she'd first shot her late father's old muzzle-loader when she was eight.

At the Katzenberger brothers' grocery store in Greenville, she saw hunters and trappers selling their wild game and made a deal with the owners to provide them quail, pheasant, rabbits and other small game which the store would then sell to restaurants in Cincinnati.

Taking up the old long rifle again, she discovered her natural skill came back to her. She made it a practice never to shoot an animal that was standing still. "They have to be running or flying to have a fair chance," she explained to her mother when describing her hunting technique. "And it makes me quick of eye and hand."

The grocery store owners later told her they preferred her game because they were head kills and the meat wasn't riddled with buckshot for a diner to break his teeth on. She remembered with fondness the Katzenberger brothers who, as a Christmas gift, gave her a can of the best gunpowder made—DuPont Eagle Ducking Black Powder, along with five pounds of shot and two boxes of percussion caps. It was like having a cake, but not wanting to eat it. More than a week passed before she could bring herself to open the tin of powder and begin using it.

At about the same time, the brothers presented her with her first, real modern gun—a Parker Brothers 16-gauge breechloader, complete with one hundred brass shells. As she thought back on it, the Katzenbergers probably had an ulterior motive for their gifts— with a good shotgun, she could bag more game for them. Game was plentiful in the Ohio woods then, and there were no limits or seasons. She studied the habits of the small animals, and recalled her father teaching her how to set traps for them. Surrounded by nature, she felt at home, and learned the identity of most of the native plants. Tramping the woods in homemade woolen skirts and leggings, she used her new gun to kill more game than ever. She cleaned and wrapped them in bunches of six or twelve and sent them by mail coach to the Katzenbergers who shipped them to hotels in Cincinnati, eighty miles away. Her ability to help support the family gave her a sense of pride. She became such a good wing shot that she began entering local shooting contests. But her skill was eventually her downfall; she won so many of the matches, the organizers finally banned her from entering. She couldn't understand why everyone considered marksmanship so difficult. "It's just like pointing your finger," she used to say.

Not long after that, friends had encouraged her to take on the touring marksman, Frank Butler. Now, here she was, twelve years later, in old England, using an assumed stage name of Oakley—a name that had a better ring through a megaphone than "Phoebe Ann Moses".

"Ma'am, I'm all done, and the guns are put away."

Annie blinked and realized she was staring at the tent wall, the embroidery hoop lying in her lap. Her former life disappeared like a dream that fades upon waking. She turned. "Oh, Matt… Yes, thanks." She smiled. You're a great help to me and Frank. But I have one further request, that I know you'll pay no attention to: Please don't call me 'ma'am'. It makes me feel like an old lady."

"But I can't call you 'Annie'."

"Why not? Everyone else does, except Colonel Cody when he refers to me as 'Little Missie'."

"Sitting Bull used to call you 'Little Miss Sureshot'."

"I know. He was a great friend."

"Why don't I call you 'Miss Oakley'?"

"Too formal. Besides, I'm not 'Miss' anybody. I'm Missus Frank Butler. Please, just call me Annie, and I'll call you Matt. I'm not even ten years older than you are. You could be my younger brother."

"Okay, Annie, but I'll have to get used to it," he said, flushing slightly. "It doesn't sound right on my tongue."

"Here, maybe this will help." She reached into a nearby jar and tossed him a stick of peppermint candy. She knew it was one of his favorites.

"Thanks." He thrust the end of the stick into his mouth and left the tent.

Annie savored the silence and solitude for several minutes. The wood shifted in the Franklin stove as the fire burned down. Since being constantly surrounded by people, she found it very relaxing and peaceful to have some time to herself. She occasionally wondered how different her life would be if she had children to care for. Or would she choose her career over domesticity and hire a nanny to care for the little ones while she toured the world? Frank had two children by a prior marriage, but it didn't appear she'd ever have any. Maybe it was for the best. She played the role of beloved "aunt" to many children she invited to her tent each week to be entertained, to socialize and be fed cookies and lemonade. Yet, she realized she could never stand being tied down by the responsibility of having her own children. Domestic chores bored her and she tended to avoid them. She and Frank had been on the road their entire marriage. She'd done just enough cooking over a gas ring in a hotel room or ironing on the flat lid of a steamer trunk to know she didn't want to make a full time job of it. She admired women who were good mothers and took satisfaction in their calling. But it wasn't for her.

She got up, opened the stove and added two more small sticks of wood from the stack beside it. Then she set a teakettle on top to boil. It was nearing four o'clock and she'd adopted the British habit of having afternoon tea. She found it helped offset a bit of a sinking spell she had in late afternoon. She pulled a shawl about her shoulders and stood close to the warmth, reflecting on why her mind was troubled. She should have been happy, carefree. And generally, she was. She had a good husband and a career doing what she loved and excelled at. She was admired by literally millions of people, and enjoyed many friends and acquaintances.

But something still nagged at her. She knew the source of her discontent, but avoided looking it in the face. It was Inspector Abberline and his damned offer. Why had that man barged into her ordered world and planted his irritating proposal? Now he stood in the wings of her mind, silently crooking a finger at her, beckoning her to come and help lend her courage and skill in stopping this phantom the police couldn't catch—this man who'd dubbed himself, Jack the Ripper, and continued to strike down women in the East End. What did he have to do with her? He was just another crazed killer. It was none of her business. But she connected his type to "The Wolves" who'd enslaved her as a child. The abuse she'd suffered was more prolonged and less deadly, but it was still abuse—the worst details of which she'd managed to blot from constant memory. How many more "Wolves" were out there, doing the same thing? This Ripper fellow was probably only the most notorious. And she'd been offered a chance to stop him. How ironic that Abberline knew nothing of her past. He'd come to her because of her fame and skill with weapons.

She didn't necessarily believe in Divine Providence or in the inevitability of events. Individuals were free to pick and choose and make decisions that affected their own and others' lives. Nothing, in her view, was predetermined.

The kettle whistled it's high pitched signal and she set a mesh strainer full of loose tea overtop her porcelain mug and poured the boiling water over it. Just breathing the steamy aroma of the spiced tea made her feel better. She desperately wanted to make herself believe everything was going to be all right—without her intervention or discomfort. Yet, deep down, she knew everything would not be all right. She sipped the tea, then took a deep breath, warming her hands on the thick cup. Could she stand by while this man continued to kill these helpless women? She had some skills that might end it. She had to make a decision once and for all.

So she did.

Before she put on another show, she would go see Abberline and offer her help. Succeed or fail, she would try, or she'd never know another day of peace.

CHAPTER 15

After supper, she told Frank in an off-hand way she had an errand to run the next morning in the city, but would return in plenty of time for the afternoon performance. This was something she often did. She usually mentioned where she was going; if she didn't, he never questioned her about it. Her comings and goings were almost always such innocent things as shopping for yard goods for a new costume, visiting Lancaster's custom gun works to examine a particular fowling piece, or occasionally even buying him a present in one of the London shops, or purchasing tickets for a play.

"Shall I have one of the boys drive you?" was all her husband asked.

"No. I'm not exactly sure where I'm going, so I'll take a cab." She knew *where* she was going, she just didn't know how to get there.

He nodded, shaking out a copy of a newspaper and leaning toward the lantern for a better view.

They'd traveled all over the United States and much of Europe already, so she knew he had no fear of her traveling alone in a large city. Some men were overprotective of their wives; he wasn't one of them. Early on in their marriage, she'd established the fact that she could take care of herself, and the ground rules were set. If she needed help, she'd ask for it.

Next morning as dawn was graying the fog, Annie hailed a Hansom cab passing along the street outside the arena. To avoid being recognized or hailed by any early risers connected with the show, and as protection from the dampness, she wore a hooded traveling cape. The driver, muffled against the breeze, reached down and swung open one of the lap doors. "Where to?"

"Scotland Yard." She stepped in and sat down snapping the door shut behind her. The driver's whip popped overhead and the two-wheeled cabriolet swung away down the street, the mist swirling around them. Annie shivered inside her cape. She'd be glad to get back home and see more of the sunshine. Winter was fast approaching here, and it promised to be wet, cold and dreary. The miasma that enveloped them was unfit to be drawn into the lungs as air, and Annie covered her face with the deep hood and breathed inside her cloak.

The iron-shod hooves rang a rhythmic clatter on the cobblestones as the horse pulled them down one street and then another, twisting and turning until Annie lost all sense of direction.

The early sun struggled, but failed, to penetrate the dense atmosphere.

The Hansom finally drew up at a nondescript red brick building, and Annie climbed out, absently handing the driver a coin.

"Mum," the driver acknowledged, touching his plug hat.

She toyed with the idea of asking him to wait, but then decided not to, as she had no idea how long she'd be. A clerk inside the main entrance directed her to the office of Inspector Abberline. As long as she kept her hood up, no one recognized her as the person whose face graced thousands of posters and handbills throughout the city.

She passed a young man who was working at a desk in an open area near several offices—evidently a shared clerk.

Hesitating at the door labeled, Chief Inspector Abberline, she took a deep breath and knocked softly. The door was ajar and swung inward.

"Enter."

She pushed inside, shoving back her hood as she did so.

Abberline looked up and thrust a desk pen into its holder.

"Miss Oakley," he greeted heartily, a wide smile stretching his mustache. "Please, do come in. Close the door."

He came out from behind the desk and pulled up an armchair for her. "Let me have your wrap." He hung the cape on the coat rack and then returned to seat himself near her.

She noted he could hardly contain his enthusiasm.

"I must say, regardless of the purpose of your visit, this is the brightest thing that's happened to me this week."

"Thanks, inspector. I hope you don't live to regret that statement." Then she paused, unsure of how to proceed. Americans had a reputation for being straightforward, so that's what she'd be. "I want to volunteer to help catch this Jack the Ripper."

"Excellent!" Color came into his face and he beamed at her. As if unable to sit still, he got up and began to pace. "Have you shared this decision with your husband and with Colonel Cody?"

"They'll know about it in due time."

He turned toward her. "Then they would not agree."

"I make my own decisions. This Ripper murders helpless women. I know what it's like to be abused. I was in slavery as a child, and I feel I should do all I can to assist in this man's capture."

"You're aware of the danger, but agree to accept the risk?"

"If I'm not aware, you'll enlighten me."

"Of course, we'll do everything humanly possible to protect you from harm, but there's an element of real danger."

"Certainly. My knees were trembling when I came in here."

"I shouldn't wonder. It's better than being overconfident." He began to pace again. "You will act as a decoy to lure this man out of hiding, so we can arrest him."

"Or kill him if you must."

"Quite so. It's very possible this ploy won't work because we're not certain why he attacks some women and not others. There seems to be no pattern, although most of the attacks have taken place on weekends."

Annie nodded.

"We'll dress you appropriately and I'll have one of the East End prostitutes coach you on how to act."

"Okay." She looked directly into his eyes as he stopped in front of her. "This won't involve wing shots or long range shooting. Why select me?"

"I approached you about this because I think you have courage and won't panic in a moment of crisis." He shrugged. "And, of course for obvious other reasons—you're young, pretty, athletic and probably the world's keenest sharpshooter, with either pistol or long gun." He pivoted and paced away several steps, hands behind his back, head down. "If the man actually makes a move to kill you," he went on in a matter-of-fact way, "he'll try to strangle you first before using the knife. That's been the pattern. Based on the autopsies, the doctors have concluded his victims were unconscious before he slashed them. I'm sure it wasn't mercy on his part. It was just easier; the women couldn't scream or struggle if they were senseless."

"What makes you think I won't flinch under pressure?"

"Because I've seen you perform incredible acts of skill before thousands of spectators without losing your composure."

"Public performance is a different kind of pressure, inspector."

"Quite right. But if you won't panic when a misstep would let down your fellow performers and disappoint a grandstand full of people, including the queen and several crowned heads of Europe, I'm certain you won't panic when your own life is at stake. Your handling of firearms is pure instinct, honed to a skill by long practice. It's automatic now. You can get a revolver into play faster and more accurately than anyone alive."

Abberline's confidence in her was amazing. Was it too late to back out of this?

"Let me tell you what I have in mind," he said, pausing in his pacing and sitting down in the chair several feet opposite her. "A special, rigid collar will be made for you that you'll wear under a neck-high blouse. It can't be crushed by hands, nor cut by the slash of a knife. The rest of you will be vulnerable, but we'll fit you with a special corset that will deflect a slash, if not a direct thrust. The Chinese tongs wear quilted padding that protects their body from most knife wounds."

"Sounds as if I'll be in armor."

"In effect, you will."

"Will this hamper my mobility?"

"I don't think so, but we'll leave that up to you, once the protective clothing is in place."

"I'll be able to select my own weapon?"

"Of course."

"After I see what I'm supposed to put on, I might modify it to be sure my movements are not hindered by anything. I've designed and made many of my own shooting outfits."

"Those were for show, not for protection. But you'll have the final say. We'll be watching your every move from a distance, and I have some men who are most adept at staying hidden. If you should be approached by a normal customer, deceived by your... profession, you're free to get rid of him as you choose."

"That will be no problem." She thought for a moment. "Will I have any idea who he is when I see him?"

"An idea only. Nothing for certain. We've compiled a composite from all the eyewitness accounts, including that of Mister Hutchinson, who apparently had the closest view of him. We think he's a local Whitechapel resident, and was probably interviewed by the police and released for lack of evidence. He's between five-foot, five and five-foot, seven in height, slender to medium build, roughly thirty-five years old, wears a small mustache that could be waxed on the ends, might be wearing a soft hat or a deerstalker, sometimes known to wear a watch chain, dressed in wools and tweeds of good make, but very well worn. Soft-spoken and superficially charming, he presents no obvious threat to women."

"That'll at least give me a general description, so I can be on the lookout."

"When can you begin? It will take us a day or so to prepare. Once you're on the street, our fishing expedition might not get any bites the first night, so we'll continue for several nights. If nothing happens then, we'll agree our attempt was a failure."

"The show closes in two days, inspector. Then we pack up and entrain for Southampton where we catch our ship. Two more performances, then I'm all yours."

Abberline rose. "Excellent. The moon is full this coming weekend. Perfect timing. Police records show there are always more crimes and bizarre behavior around the time of the full moon. The ancient Romans even noted that their 'luna' had an obvious negative influence on men's actions. Hence, our word, 'lunatic'. If a full moon can pull tides in the ocean, it can certainly pull an unbalanced mind over the edge. The full moon might bust be the final bit of bait we need."

TWANG!

The Bowie knife quivered in the barn wall, its point buried an inch in the crudely chalked target.

Matt and Crowfoot moved up and the Indian wiggled the knife loose from the splintered wood.

"Okay, lemme try it now," Matt said, holding out his hand. Crowfoot handed over the knife, handle first.

The two young men backed off to a line they'd scuffed in the dirt fifteen paces from the rear wall of the horse barn.

Matt hefted the knife, feeling its considerable weight and realizing the blade and the handle were nearly balanced. He was adept at throwing a baseball, but this was an entirely different skill. He grasped the weapon by the end of the blade, being careful not to wrap his fingers around the sharp edge. He leaned forward slightly at the waist, whipped the knife around in a sidearm motion and let fly.

THUD!

The Bowie rattled off the planks to the ground.

"Damn!" he muttered. "I can't seem to get the hang of it."

They walked up to retrieve it. "You put some kind of spin on it?" Matt asked.

"I get skill from my people," Crowfoot said. "The Sioux have knives before we have white man's guns."

"Not in your lifetime," Matt countered. "Besides, you don't inherit a skill; talent, maybe, but not skill." He picked up the knife and wiped off the dusty blade on his pants leg. He handed it over, haft first. "Lemme see you do that again."

They retreated to their mark, about forty feet away. "You reckon it would help if I moved closer?" Matt asked.

Crowfoot shook his head. "Start this way," he said, whipping the knife downward into the ground about three feet from his foot. The blade buried itself half of its length. The Indian pulled it out, wiping off the dirt. "Practice this way. Knife make only one and a half turns before it sticks." He handed Matt the weapon.

Matt whipped it down and managed to make the point stick two out of three attempts.

"Better," Crowfoot said. "Blade heavier than handle, so it should land first."

Matt moved up to thirty feet from the back wall of the barn and took aim at the lopsided chalked circle on the boards.

CLANG!

The knife hit, handle first, and bounced off. "Lemme try it a few more times," he said, running to pick it up. "Felt like I almost had it that time."

He worked his way closer and threw from twenty-five feet, then eighteen. One of his throws hit point first, but without enough force to stick. "I think I got it now."

"No wonder white men had to have thundersticks," Crowfoot observed, standing with his arms folded and lapsing into his *faux* dialect.

Matt ignored the condescending grin. He threw three more times with the same result. He had yet to make the knife stick in the dry, splintered wood. "What am I doing wrong?"

141

"Like this," Crowfoot said, taking the knife. He cocked his elbow. "Throw from ear, not sidearm." He whipped the knife forward with an arm motion that was a blur. The point stuck. "More speed."

Matt tried again, throwing with a quick, short motion and all his strength. The knife stuck and quivered. "Ahhh! Like an overhand pitcher!"

"Now you get it," Crowfoot said, walking up, placing the fingers of one hand on either side of the blade and wrenching it loose with his other hand. "You keep practicing. Someday you be as good as Indian."

"Not in a hundred years," Matt conceded.

During the next half hour, before his arm grew tired, he managed to make the Bowie stick in or near the target a dozen times.

Crowfoot glanced at the sun. "I must go put on warpaint for show," he said, finally taking his knife and wiping off the blade and elkhorn handle and shoving it into its beaded sheath at his belt.

"Yeah, Annie will be looking for me, too," Matt said as the boys started back toward the tents and corrals. "Meet me after supper."

Crowfoot nodded.

"Crofe! Crofe! Come here!"

The 19-year old Sioux looked around, then threw down the handful of straw he was using to wipe down the sweaty flanks and back of his paint pony. "What?"

Matt gestured again. "Got something to tell ya."

Crowfoot moved toward his friend and the two of them stepped out of the busy staging area behind a stack of hay bales. "What so important?" the Indian asked. "I must cool down and water my pony before we go to the mess tent."

"This won't take a minute." Matt looked around to be sure they were out of earshot of everyone. "You gotta promise on whatever you hold sacred you won't breathe a word of this."

Crowfoot's obsidian eyes regarded him curiously.

"You promise?"

"My word is good."

"I just overheard Annie and Frank arguing."

"So?"

"You'll never guess what it was about."

Crowfoot didn't try.

"Annie told him she was going to help Scotland Yard trap Jack the Ripper."

Crowfoot's eyes went wide. "She lose her mind?"

"Frank was really hot about it. Called her all kinds of an idiot and a fool. But she stood her ground and didn't back down an inch. She went to see the Chief Inspector this morning."

Crowfoot shrugged. "No matter. Cody will not allow it."

"The show ends after tomorrow's performance, so all he can do is threaten to cancel her contract."

"How Annie help police?"

"The inspector came here a few days ago and asked her to act as a decoy to lure this killer out of hiding. She and her husband and Cody all turned him down. But she's been thinking about it. I knew something was on her mind yesterday; she didn't act right."

"The Ripper's knife is sharp and quick," Crowfoot said.

"Yeah, but Annie's determined to do it."

Crowfoot was silent for a moment. "We not let her do this alone."

"She told Frank the police'll be watching her."

"Ripper fast, good with knife," the Indian said. "We must follow her, too."

"What if we get in the way, and she gets killed?"

"We not let that happen. Find out when and where. We'll be there in shadows."

Beth Hampton and Annie Oakley sat alone at a table in The Three Bells two nights later. Chief Inspector Abberline leaned on the bar, sipping a bitters, and pretended to ignore the nearby women.

"Now listen, Annie, you have to forget you're gentry," Beth said. "For now, you're just a common working girl, like the rest of us. Pretend you have to attract a man or two to earn your doss money tonight, or you'll be sleeping in some doorway."

Beth was pushing forty, graying blond, short hair, rosy cheeked and tending to plump, although with a full figure that even Abberline could eye with appreciation.

Annie nodded. This might be more complicated than she imagined. Maybe Abberline should have hired an actress from one of the music halls to play this part.

"All of us can accept or turn away any man we want," Beth was saying, leaning across the table. "So don't feel that you must say 'yes' every time you get a proposition." She hesitated. "A bit of advice, just between us girls. In case you think you have a bite from the killer, and want to continue bringing him on, you have to play the role out—or nearly so. If you flip up your skirts and lean up against a wall, these men don't know where they're sticking it. Most of them have been at the sauce and their sails are luffing into the wind, anyway. Grip his pizzle between your thighs. It's usually over in a minute. I've been working the streets for ten years, and I doubt I've actually been penetrated more than a dozen times."

"Really?" Annie tried not to look surprised. There were certainly tricks to every trade. She glanced at Abberline and noticed him eyeing her critically from the bar over a foamy glass of beer. She was embarrassed by this conversation, even though he was certainly too far away to hear their words above the noise in the pub. She knew when she volunteered to assist that it would take a great effort of will to suppress her extreme modesty. Frank was the only man she'd ever been intimate with. In public, especially when she was performing, she even went to the trouble of hooking the hem of her skirt to her leggings. This tether ensured that her skirt would not fly up in the windy arena even if she were turning flips, walkovers, standing on her head to shoot, or drilling targets from her bicycle or horseback.

144

She was far too young to be thinking of death, but she'd put herself in a position where she might never see her next birthday. She made a silent resolution that the very next day she would seek out a female mortician—if such a thing existed in London—and sign a contract, if necessary, to ensure that a woman would prepare her body for burial if the worst happened and The Ripper should get her. The image of her nude, mutilated body would not be splashed all over the tabloids. And no male undertaker would touch her. She would extract a promise from Inspector Abberline that no autopsy would be performed on her. The panicky thought of being seen immodestly in public, dead or alive, terrified her nearly as much as being murdered by this insane killer.

"Since this is your first night, I'll walk out with you if you want," Beth was offering.

"What?" She was jarred back to the present. "Oh…yes, thank you. That would be good, just to get the hang of it," Annie said.

Beth glanced at the big clock above the bar. "Shall we go? It's nearly eleven."

Annie rose and the two women sauntered outside. The streets of Whitechapel were still crawling with many pedestrians, most seemingly bent on some errand or other, but others just loafing in doorways or under gas lamps, talking, smoking.

A cool, damp breeze was blowing and Annie noted the full moon overhead, being shut off and on by scudding clouds. She swallowed. Her mouth and throat were dry. "Do you have a mint?"

"Sure do. They make your breath sweet. Glad you thought of that."

Beth nodded and spoke to several women and a couple of men she knew. "Don't walk so fast, Annie," she whispered. "You can't seem to be in a hurry. You don't have anywhere to go. You're just out for a stroll. You can looked interested, open, but not too eager."

"Like this?" Annie slowed and affected a seductive walk.

"Almost. Not so obvious."

Annie tried to flow along the sidewalk, allowing her body

145

to flex and bend easily, but it was difficult with the padded corset gripping her midsection.

"Don't worry, dearie, it takes practice."

"Somehow I don't think I'll be at this long enough to get good at it."

Beth giggled. "I can't believe I'm training the famous Annie Oakley to be a prostitute."

"Sshhh! Not so loud," Annie whispered, head down. She couldn't bend her head very far because of the rigid wooden neck ring sewn into the stand-up collar of her frilly blouse. The voluminous petticoats made her feel overdressed, and she almost wished she'd left off the pantaloons beneath. But every additional layer of clothing would help protect her, should it come to that. The thin frock coat over the blouse hid the shoulder holster strapped beneath. Instead of leather, the strap and holster were fashioned of a heavy white canvas whose color blended with the blouse, so as to be nearly invisible in dim light. Even the bird's head pistol grip was ivory. After much study and deliberation, she'd selected a nickel-plated, five-shot, .44 caliber Merwin Hulbert, made by Allen & Hopkins Company. It had a three-and-a-half inch barrel, and the hammer spur folded down to keep from snagging when the gun was drawn. It could be fired as single or double action. She'd greased the inside of the canvas holster to facilitate a faster draw, but had to be careful she didn't bend over too far and allow the gun to slip out.

Two years earlier she'd bought it to use in her act, but then discovered it was too short and powerful to make a good target pistol. She admired the beautiful design and workmanship. A gunsmith with the show told her it was probably the best revolver made. With her natural skill, it didn't take long to become thoroughly accustomed to its heft and feel. She practiced for two days until she had complete command and it felt as natural in her hand as her other show guns. She'd carefully oiled it until the action was smooth and effortless. She was certain it would perform flawlessly if she could get to it quick enough. That would be the critical factor. Would she have enough warning? Knowing when to draw and fire would be crucial.

She dared not shoot some unoffending customer who was trying to rent her body. Yet, if she hesitated only a split second, it could be too late.

She licked her dry lips, wondering how this deadly game would end.

CHAPTER 16

The two women sashayed along Hanbury Street, then turned right onto Spital Street.

"Ah, Ruth," Beth said, pausing to greet a friend.

"Not much going tonight," Ruth said.

"Ruth, this is my friend, Constance, a new girl who just moved here from America."

"Pleased to meet'ya," Ruth said, eyeing Annie as if more competition wasn't welcome. "You know what's been going on here?"

"I know."

"Well, we're not catching any business standing around in a group," Ruth said abruptly, moving on without a backward glance.

Beth and Annie continued walking slowly to Buxton Street, then turned right and ambled in a large, rough rectangle around Baker's Row. On each corner, the ornately-lettered street names showed up distinctly in the glow of the gas lamps.

Where are they? Annie wondered. *If the police are watching me, they're well hidden. Why did I agree to do this? I'm out of my element.*

But it was too late for second thoughts. She was into it now, and would see it through, come what may. The two women meandered along in silence. When they turned onto Old Montague Street, a clock in the distant Spitalfields tower began to strike.

"Midnight," Beth said. "The witching hour." She laughed.

"We'll see some workingmen getting off late shift now."

Sure enough, within ten minutes, a stocky man in a soft cap stopped Beth. He said something quietly to her while Annie held back out of earshot.

"Why, yes." She turned to Annie. "I'll see you later. Back at the Three Bells." She moved away, holding the man's arm.

Annie continued on alone, feeling much more vulnerable without her companion. In the bright moonlight and inky shadows, she noticed men walking singly, and in twos and threes, going to and from jobs at places like the produce market, bakeries, warehouses. Perhaps some were dock workers and night watchmen. She could see no one's face; they were dark figures only, and none of them approached her. Did she not give off an aura of an available woman? Or did they have their own families to go home to? Beth was right; this was a job that required a lot of experience. And it was a most dangerous job—subject to disease and violence, dealing intimately with total strangers, many of them drunk.

She walked with her head down, picking her way across the street, stepping carefully to keep from slipping on the wet cobblestones. She thought of all the women in Whitechapel who were trying to keep body and soul together with this ancient occupation. To escape the fear and hopelessness of such a perilous life, many of her "sisters under the skin" slid into drugs and alcohol, creating even more problems for themselves.

"Hey, you wanta go?"

"Oh!" She jumped sideways, startled, her heart leaping at the sudden voice at her elbow.

"Didn't mean to scare you." The man stopped, holding out one hand.

"That's okay...I didn't see you..." she gasped, her heart rate beginning to slow.

"Are you up for it?" he asked.

"Yes." She scanned him in the bright moonlight. Did he fit the description? No. He was too big by half. At least a two-hundred pound man, dressed in rough work clothes, smelling of fish.

149

"Where? You have a favorite place?"

She had to get rid of this man quickly. "We haven't agreed on a price."

"Figured it was the going rate."

"Half a crown."

"What? I didn't want to buy it—just rent it."

"That's the rate."

"You're working the wrong neighborhood. I wouldn't pay that much for a virgin."

"Take it or leave it."

"Don't get huffy. You got a funny way o'talking. You ain't from these parts," he grumbled, moving away. "You'll learn soon enough." He melted into the shadows.

Annie found she was perspiring under the heavy clothing. She slipped a hand beneath her coat and touched the reassuring ivory grip of the Merwin Hulbert pocket pistol.

"Crofe, she's picked up a client," Matt said to his Sioux friend as the two of them crouched behind a fence in the side yard close to a darkened brick building a half block away.

"Big man," the Indian grunted, sliding a Bowie knife from a scabbard on his belt.

"Hold it. That might not be The Ripper."

"Police not around."

"How do you know? Bet there's a constable or two nearby. Maybe even Chief Inspector Abberline."

"I do not feel them," Crowfoot whispered.

"Huh! You're so far removed from your Indian roots, you'd have a hard time sensing if you were barefoot."

"Insults not hurt Crowfoot."

Matt grinned in the dark as the pair continued watching Annie and the big man conversing in the middle of the street.

A few seconds later, the man threw up his hands and lumbered off.

"She got rid of him."

"If she keeps doing that, and the Ripper is anywhere around, he'll get wise to her," Matt said. "But she can't really take on paying customers. This is all for show."

They waited until Annie had strolled on another two hundred yards before they moved to follow. Crowfoot crept along in soundless moccasins, but had shed his Sioux show garb in favor of dark cotton pants and a faded blue shirt. His long black hair was fixed in a short, thick braid in back and he wore a black felt hat.

Matt was dressed in worn Levis, red woolen shirt and brown felt hat. Neither boy was encumbered by a coat.

Chief Inspector Abberline and one uniformed constable were also observing Annie from the other side of the street. Constable Carrington was the best marksman in the precinct, and carried a short, lever action carbine, .32-20 caliber. If The Ripper showed up and they couldn't get to Annie quick enough, he was to try a shot as a last resort to save her life. In place of his helmet, the constable had donned a close-fitting blue woolen stocking cap that effectively hid his blond hair.

Abberline had left his long ulster at The Three Bells, and wore a thick sweater. On his feet were the rubber-soled canvas shoes he wore at the athletic club. They were light, flexible and gripped better than his leather-soled street shoes. His black felt hat shaded his eyes and face.

"Inspector, we could get a better view and angle of fire from that iron balcony up there," Carrington said, pointing at the stairway leading up to the second floor overhang on a lodging house.

"As long as she's moving, we have to be mobile. It'd take too long to get down from there if something happened out of range," Abberline answered softly.

Keeping to the deep black shadows cast by the full moon, the two lawmen slunk along behind a row of buildings, trying not to lose sight of her for more than a few seconds at a time.

"Wish I could signal her to walk slower," Abberline panted as the two men slid up to the corner of a warehouse and peeked around.

"Only one man's approached her so far," the constable said, lowering the carbine.

The Spitalfields clock tower chimed the quarter hour, then the half hour and Annie continued to stroll the mostly empty streets—along Thrawl Street, then across Osborn to Finch Street.

Abberline noted she seemed to move with a much more relaxed gait, similar to the other prostitutes. Now and then another woman would appear, walking alone on the other side of the street. One at a time, three more were accosted and disappeared into darkened alleyways.

The two men trailed Annie in silence and blackness until nearly three o'clock when, as instructed by Abberline, she worked her way back to her starting point at The Three Bells.

"Appears we've had no luck tonight," Abberline said as their decoy reentered the pub. "You're dismissed to go back to your beat."

"Yes, sir." The young rifleman faded into the darkness.

A good man, Abberline thought. Disciplined, efficient, and a crack shot.

The Chief Inspector went into the pub.

"Closing time, gentlemen!" The barman jangled his keys, ready to call it a night. "Drink up and be off to your beds."

The last stroke of three echoed from the distant clock tower.

"Harry, I'll get permission for you to stay open until eight in the morning for the next week. We need your place to meet."

"Fine by me, inspector. I could use the extra business from all the fellas who get off at four. Lots of men work odd hours in the East End," the balding barkeep said.

Annie and Beth sat at a table, heads together, ignoring them, and conversing in low tones.

No word passed between Abberline and Annie, but, by prearrangement, she was to leave, pick up a waiting cab the inspector had hired just outside, and go back to the Metropole Hotel where

Cody had reserved a room for her and Frank Butler.

The Wild West Show had packed up the day before, and the train pulled out for Southampton this morning. Cody moved into the Metropole for a few days, indicating he'd catch up with the show before they embarked.

Matt and Crowfoot had purposely missed the train to deal themselves into this dangerous experiment. They'd used their savings to put themselves up in a cheap lodging house for a few days before they were forced to leave for Southampton, or risk being stranded this side of the big water. No one knew they had knowledge of Annie's role as decoy.

The next night was a repeat of the first, except that Annie extended her time on the street until 4:00 a.m. By then, Abberline was beginning to fear The Ripper had somehow sensed a trap and gone into hiding. Yet, the killer had previously allowed several weeks to pass between murders. Abberline redoubled his efforts with Constable Carrington to be sure they were not observed.

The third night of fishing also produced no results.

Abberline sat in The Three Bells just after midnight nursing a pint of bitters. The radical experiment had started out with high hopes. They were now beginning to fade as each night passed. Perhaps the horrible Mary Kelly murder and dismemberment had sated the monster's blood lust for now, or possibly for good. Even if the man wasn't caught, if this was the end of his atrocities, so be it. Abberline would heave a great sigh of relief and be satisfied. Not every case came to a neat conclusion or was solved. If it faded away like the Black Death of earlier times, he'd be grateful.

Annie and Beth came in and sat down at the table with Abberline. The pub was crowded just after midnight, and the hum of conversation, laughter and clinking of glassware made it possible for them to talk in normal low tones and not be overheard.

"Did you really say that?" Beth laughed as they pulled up their chairs. "Annie—I mean, Constance—you've really caught on

153

quick."

"What's this?" Abberline asked.

"Well, last night I had four prospective clients," Annie said. "I knew none of them fit the Ripper's description, so in case anyone was watching, I took them into the alley but told them it was my time of the month. Two of them I even paid a shilling each to go about their business and keep their mouths shut, or I'd have them arrested for attacking me. With this Ripper scare on, they took to their heels, so they wouldn't be accused. Likely went looking for fair game to spend my shilling on."

Abberline smiled. At least Annie was not as tense as she'd been a few nights before. He hoped she didn't get too relaxed, thinking this was all a game. She'd decided not to wear a hat during her nightly forays. Abberline thought the look of her dark brown glossy hair, flowing to her shoulders, was an added allure. But he had to admit he was thinking like a normal man. And The Ripper had shown he was anything but normal. If Annie wanted to cover her head, she'd use the shawl she wore about her shoulders. In case of emergency, she could use the knit shawl to entangle the arms or knife of an assailant.

"Ladies, before we started this, I resolved to give it a go for eight straight nights," Abberline said. "If we can't lure him out of hiding in that time, over the course of the full moon, it's not likely to happen at all." He looked at one and then the other. "This is the fourth night of our quest, one night past the full moon. But the moon won't be visible tonight." He jerked his head toward the door. "A real pea-souper out there now. I've seen these before. It's not likely to clear off before noon, if then."

"Inspector, I have a suggestion," Annie said. "Since several of these murders were committed in the darkest hour or two just before dawn, why don't I start out after two o'clock and go until daylight? Sort of vary up the routine. Maybe he's on the prowl in the wee hours."

"Good idea. It's worth a try. But this fog's so thick, don't move too fast, and try to stay near the street lamps as much as you can, so I don't lose you."

"Okay."

"I'll leave you two alone now. I'll be at the bar. Slip out of here a bit after two and I'll follow." He nodded to them, got up and edged through the crowd, thinking it was nearly as smoky inside as out. He helped himself to a pickled herring from the free lunch. The salty food was guaranteed to stoke a thirst, but he didn't care. His mind was on other things. He tried to count how many people were in on this ploy. He and Annie and Beth, Buffalo Bill Cody and Frank Butler, and Constable Carrington. As far as he knew, that was all—the minimum number required to make this work. He'd sworn them all to secrecy, and had no reason to think anyone would betray his trust. He knew Beth was bursting to tell someone, so he'd assured her she could say anything she wanted after it was over and the experiment had failed. If it succeeded, then she'd likely be a celebrity.

He moved toward the front window, but the outside light over the pub's door penetrated only a few feet into the dense fog that had flowed in just before dark. As the seasons changed from Autumn to Winter, the warm and cold air often clashed over the sprawling city, roiling down an impenetrable fog. At the far end of the block where the lamplighter on stilts had earlier touched off the gas flame, the streetlight struggled to produce a fuzzy glow in the murk. This would make it nearly impossible for him and Constable Carrington to keep a constant surveillance. The weather might just provide the edge The Ripper needed. Abberline cringed at the thought that'd been nagging him—what if the killer ignored Annie and picked on some other victim entirely? There was no way the police could assign a surreptitious guard to every one of several hundred prostitutes in Whitechapel. Again he wondered if Janelle Stafford's assessment of female musk attracting male killers had any validity. Women knew a lot more than men about things like that. But he'd never heard of any scientific experiments being conducted in that area—unless it had to do with wild animals. Where humans were concerned, it was very likely just another of those folk tales, like the widely-held belief that an image of the killer was recorded on the dead victim's eyes.

As Abberline stood staring out at the swirling mist, he almost wished this night would pass as uneventfully as the previous three. Did the Ripper work in fog? He didn't recall any of the murders being committed in a thick fog. There'd been some late night and early morning mist, but nothing this heavy. Perhaps this murk would be a hindrance to the slasher in making a quick escape. Anyone attempting to commit murder tonight would have to get away in a waiting carriage or else be very familiar with the byways of Whitechapel if fleeing on foot. He was convinced the Ripper lived somewhere close by and went afoot. He could hardly have hailed a Hansom if he were covered in blood. Besides, all the cab drivers had been questioned more than once. If The Ripper lived in the neighborhood, the police had certainly scooped him into their net—unless he'd quickly left the city and maybe the country right after each murder to avoid the resulting search. That possibility gave even more credence to Queen Victoria's theory that it could be a butcher from one of the cattle boats on the Thames.

He drained his beer. A dull headache was coming on—as it usually did when he spun a mental go-round with all the possible suspects. The description he'd given Annie was very likely accurate, leaning heavily as it did upon Hutchinson's description. It was the best they had to go on, and it blended with the general descriptions of most other witnesses.

Bong...Bong!

The muffled hour of two struck from the Spitalfield clock tower. As the last stroke sounded, Annie, Beth and another prostitute rose from their table. As Abberline watched, the three women pushed out the door and were immediately folded into the swirling white mist.

CHAPTER 17

The three women had gone only a half block in the thick fog when Beth stopped. "We'd best split up here. Olive and I have to earn our doss money."

Olive wasn't in on the secret, so Beth was making sure it stayed that way. "Sorry to leave you alone, Annie, but I think it's best for all of us."

"You're right," Annie said. "In case you come up short, take this." She pressed a coin into Beth's hand, then handed one to Olive.

"God bless you, Annie," Beth said, apparently forgetting Annie's cover name of Constance. "I'm going to miss seeing you around here. And not just because of this. I really like you."

"Yes, I have to leave for America," Annie said, for Olive's sake. But she had to blink back real tears and was glad for the darkness and the fog. Her throat constricted, and she finally managed to say, "I'll see you back at the pub come daylight. We'll get some breakfast." She gave Beth's hand a quick squeeze and Beth faded from sight and touch.

Annie stood still a few moments, trying to get her bearings, and feeling as she did one night on the deck of the steamer that brought the show from New York. They'd been fogbound in the North Atlantic, and she recalled the sensation of being the only person aboard a ghost ship that was floating in space. She had that same feeling now. A carriage horse clopped along the street only a few rods away, but she could see nothing of it and could hardly tell which direction it was headed because of the distorted sound.

She began walking. With no watch she'd rely on the clock tower to chime the hours and quarter hours. It would seem like a long time until daylight. She'd never really thought of what a handicap lack of vision would be. In order to stay on the sidewalk, she fixed her gaze on the ball of fuzzy light from the gas street lamp on the next corner and walked toward it. Abberline would never be able to keep her in sight tonight. He should have given her a lantern, but it was too late for that now. On the other hand, she didn't have to worry about The Ripper either. Nearing the street light, she could just make out the dark silhouette of a man and a woman crossing the intersection and heard their subdued voices. At least it was good to know that others were abroad in the fog. She wasn't completely isolated. She had to get a grip on her emotions and concentrate on filling time until daylight. To that end, she let her mind relax and drift, conjuring up scenes from past shows, the cheering crowds, the long train rides, soaking in a hot tub of water in her collapsing canvas bath tub, eating in the mess tent with Frank and all the cast members of the show—cowboys, stock handlers, Indians, roustabouts.

She recalled the thrill of being introduced to Queen Victoria and her royal party in their box. She, the poor little girl from Greenville, Ohio, the tomboy Phoebe Ann Moses, actually curtsying to the little elderly lady who headed the British Empire. How could such a thing have come to pass within a few short years? All because of her poverty and her need to hunt to help her family survive. Yet it was more than that. She'd been born with an extraordinary talent that few had been given. She had a rare hand/eye coordination. It was a combination of talent, opportunity and necessity. Circumstances had meshed at just the right time for her to become Annie Oakley. Her marriage to Frank Butler, their touring show, the fact that Nate Salsbury had seen her shoot just as Buffalo Bill Cody had lost his sharpshooter. It was all too complicated for her. She would just continue to do the best she could in whatever situations she found herself, and pray that God would take care of the rest.

She knew her Quaker mother, Ruth, would be horrified,

scandalized if she could see her now—walking the streets like a common prostitute, trying to lure a killer. With any luck, her mother would never know. Annie's memories of her childhood mistreatment by "The Wolves" was the real reason she'd accepted Abberline's proposal.

She shook her head. *Forget all that. Concentrate on something else to fill the time until I can return to the pub and catch a cab back to Frank at the Metropole.*

She moved under the streetlamp and felt for the curb with her foot. She stepped off to cross, and her ankle rolled on a rounded cobblestone. "Oh!" She flung out her arms as she started to fall, but was suddenly caught around the waist by a strong arm.

"Oops!" a male voice said. "I got you, Missie." Someone pulled her upright again.

At the sound of the name, "Missie", she instantly thought of Cody's pet name for her. But this wasn't the tall, elegant Bill Cody. This man was hardly five foot, seven.

Suddenly flustered, she struggled to find her voice. "I… thank you, sir. I…uh, turned my ankle."

"Glad I was here to help." He doffed his soft felt hat.

They still stood within the circle of dim light cast by the gas street lamp, and she saw a neatly groomed man with dark hair and mustache. A cape hid most of his clothing, except for a gold watch chain stretching from a vest pocket.

Her stomach tensed as she looked at him.

"Is your ankle all right?" he asked. "You can lean on me if you wish."

A silent alarm bell rang in the back of her mind. Yet, this man was a gentleman, judging from his look and manners. He couldn't have been stalking her; the fog was too thick. He just happened to be at the right place at the right time to keep her from falling.

"I…think I'm all right now. Thank you."

"A woman shouldn't be on the street alone at this time of night," he continued. "It's not safe."

While Annie was trying to form an answer, he said, "On the

159

other hand, if you're a working girl, I might have a proposition for you."

Was this the man? He fit the general description. She could not afford to turn him away, just in case. Her heart began to beat so forcefully, it nearly shook her frame, and she was sure he could see her trembling.

"Actually, I'd like to hear your proposal," she heard herself saying.

"I pay well if you're in the mood." His voice was smooth, cultured.

"That's good," Annie said. Where was Abberline—and his constable? She coughed loudly, hoping to signal him, but knew the sound would be muffled within a few yards. "A tickle in my throat," she said. "Must be the dampness."

"Do you have a room nearby?" the man asked.

"No. It's a long way from here." She was thinking of her room at the Metropole, wishing she were there with Frank right now.

"You're so very beautiful, I hate not being able to see you in the dark," he said.

"We don't need to go into an alley or a courtyard," Annie said. "The fog is so thick, no one can see us."

"Someone might come along the sidewalk," the soothing voice said.

She nearly cringed when he took her hand and began leading her out of the gas lamplight.

Then they were into the thick fog and he didn't slow down, moving as if he knew where he was going.

A breeze stirred and shredded the heaviest fog, enabling her to make out a slight offset, or alcove, in the front wall of a brick building. "Here's a spot," she said. At least it was right on the street.

"Yes, a good place," he agreed.

She would have to pretend to go through with it to make him reveal himself—*if* this was the man.

Just as she turned away from him to brace her hands against the wall, she noticed he carried something in a small leather packet in his left hand. *Where was Abberline?* She bent at the waist, and placed her palms against the bricks, but kept most of her weight on her feet.

She felt him fumbling with her skirt and voluminous petticoats.

She was trying to plan her next move, but he struck before she was ready. Throwing his weight against her bottom, he knocked her headfirst into the brick wall, bending her wrist and scraping her forehead. She sucked in a breath to scream, but his hands shot out and he locked his fingers around her throat.

"Damned dirty whore!" he hissed as the wooden ring in her collar stopped his grip, giving her a couple of seconds.

"*HELP! MURDER!*" she shrieked. The fog muffled her scream like a feather pillow.

His grip crushed the wooden ring as easily as an eggshell, driving splinters through the collar and into her neck. She felt a stinging sensation and then the horrifying pressure of his fingers like iron bands.

She twisted away from him, stumbling on her long skirts and falling onto her back next to the wall. He was on top of her like a striking cobra, but not before her hand shot inside her coat and gripped the pistol. But his weight landed on her arm and she couldn't draw the weapon. His incredible strength was squeezing her windpipe and she saw spots before her eyes.

He wasn't a big man. Adrenaline strength rushed through her and she bucked like a wild horse. Her third lunge threw him upward a few inches. In that instant she yanked out the gun, thrust the short barrel into his gut and pulled the trigger.

A muffled explosion and she felt the air rush out of him. He rolled off sideways. She hesitated for a heartbeat, knowing she'd just shot a man. When she fired blindly again, the bullet hit a trash can, but the muzzle flash lit up a pair of glittering eyes and a descending knife blade. The blade slashed through her corset, but thick padding and whalebone stays caught the blade and saved her abdomen. She fired instinctively where he should have been, but the bullet smashed a window, and the muzzle flash showed only empty space. He was gone into the fog.

Something whizzed past her head and she heard a gasp, then the clatter of a blade into the corner. She whirled toward the gasp and fired again. But he wasn't there and she heard a pair of shoe soles slapping on wet pavement, receding.

She fired rapidly, emptying the gun at the sound, but the running steps continued, fading into silence.

Ten minutes earlier:

"Damnation! I lost her, Carrington," Abberline said.

"Stand still and listen."

The two men stopped and Abberline strained to hear any sounds of footsteps. But the cottony tendrils of fog encased them in a soundless cocoon.

"There!" the constable said, pointing. "Under the streetlight."

He couldn't see her distinctly, but knew it was Annie by her uncovered head and the shiny dark hair. She paused in the light and looked around, as if reluctant to move on.

"Wish she'd stay right there," Abberline murmured.

"It'd be easier for The Ripper to find her, too."

"I wouldn't be surprised if he could see in the dark like a cat," Abberline replied.

They fell silent, watching her dark silhouette. Finally, she stepped off the curb, took two steps and started to fall. A man appeared out of the dark and caught her before she went down.

"Ah!" Abberline was startled.

Standing just at the outer edge of the circle of light, partially obscured by the fog, the man and Annie appeared to be engaged in conversation, although their voices couldn't be heard from where Abberline and Carrington stood in the dark a half block away.

"She's attracted a client," Carrington said.

"Wish I could tell if it's the client we're looking for."

A minute later, the man took her hand and they moved away across the street and disappeared.

"Let's move closer," Abberline said. "But be very cautious. We don't want to walk right up on them if they stop."

The lawmen carefully advanced forty steps down the street in the general direction of the vanished couple.

Finally Abberline put out a hand to stop his companion. They backed up against the wall to allow a lone woman to pass them. Then voices sounded and two workmen passed, one of them smoking a pipe. The men passed, deep in conversation. Aromatic pipe smoke perfumed the air.

A half minute of silence ensued.

Sounds of a scuffle reached them. The muffled *BOOM!* of a gunshot. Then, *BOOM!...BOOM!* Two louder blasts. A hesitation. *BOOM! BOOM!*

Before the last shots were even fired, Abberline and Carrington were dashing toward the explosions. Abberline saw the last two muzzles flashes dimly through the murk.

A running figure sprinted along the edge of the street light and into the fog again.

Carrington opened his shuttered lantern and the two men slid to a stop by Annie who was still sitting on the sidewalk.

"You hurt?"

"No. He's getting away!" she rasped. "I shot him in the stomach."

"Stay here and help her, constable," Abberline snapped. "I'm going after him."

He dashed away, drawing his Adams from its holster. He sprinted across the street, dodging a carriage that nearly ran him down. Which way? He slid to a halt on the wet stones and listened. The faint smacking of shoe soles on pavement. To his left. He sprinted toward the sound, wishing he had a bullseye lantern, but then realized the light would only reflect from the thick fog—not penetrate it.

He paused again, and the sound of running steps grew fainter.

163

How could a man gutshot run so fast? Or was it the fog shifting the sound?

Abberline took off again. It had to be The Ripper. No one else would have reason to be running so fast this time of night in a dense fog. The man had only a ten-second head start. Abberline turned down the next street, and saw the fleeing man, black cape flying like batwings, flash past the gas lamp on the next corner.

Abberline holstered his pistol and redoubled his efforts. His hat flew off, but he ignored it and kept running. The Ripper could duck into some dark corner or alley and ambush him as he flew past. But he apparently was armed only with his infamous knife, or he would've defended himself with a gun when Annie fired. All the shots Abberline heard were from the same gun.

At the next corner he paused to listen, trying to hear over the sound of his own harsh breathing. Hollow thunder of feet pounding on wooden stairs—close by. Abberline whirled and raced back a few rods. He found an outside stairway to the second floor and roof of a building he'd just passed. A dim figure was moving over the top of a ladder onto the roof.

He sucked in a deep breath and leapt up the stairs two at a time, but paused when he reached the ladder that was fastened to the wall beside the second story door. Thumping of steps across the flat roof above. He climbed the six steps up the ladder and peeked over. Blackness. But he heard the flutter of a cape on the far side. He threw a leg over the brick balustrade and carefully crept across the tarred roof toward the spot he'd heard the flapping. Damn the fog! He was like a blind man. But it had to be just as bad for The Ripper. How could anyone keep going like this with a lead slug in his belly? He had to be running on pure adrenaline. And he wouldn't be fleeing so fast if he didn't know he was being pursued. Apparently trying to reach a safe haven before he collapsed from his wound.

Abberline reached the far side of the roof and paused again. Nothing. He put his hands on the brick parapet to climb over, and felt something warm and sticky. He sniffed his fingers. Fresh blood. Then he heard the sounds of someone scuffing along a ledge a few feet below.

"Hold it! You won't get away!" he yelled into the fog.

No reply. He heard a thud and a clatter, followed by the sibilant sliding of dislodged roof tiles, then a smashing on the courtyard below.

"You're under arrest! Give up while you're still alive!" Abberline yelled. A window banged open in the building across the narrow gap. "What's going on out there?" a voice shouted.

Had The Ripper fallen? No. Someone was scrambling up the opposite roof.

"This is crazy!" Abberline muttered, throwing a leg over the edge of the brick balustrade. He climbed over and let himself down onto the narrow ledge.

His quarry wasn't far ahead; he could hear him scrabbling up the slick tiles on the next roof, and then saw a flicker of the cape disappearing behind a chimney pot. He could even hear heavy, harsh breathing. *Got you now!* Abberline thought.

But maybe not. He didn't fancy leaping across to that steep pitched roof. Instead, he opted to slide down the drain pipe and head him off. But what if the man continued on across the rooftops, and didn't descend? Or just stopped to rest where he was, and then retraced his steps? The fog was The Ripper's ally. There were hundreds of places he could hide. Unless the man was dying of his gunshot wound, he'd get away again and never be found.

All these thoughts flashed through his mind as he paused to figure his next move.

There was no sound. The Ripper must have stopped as well.

"Who's there? What's going on?" came a tremulous voice from a window hardly a dozen feet away. Startled, Abberline slid along the narrow ledge to the corner of the building, hoping the man in the window didn't see him. He felt for the downspout, found it and eased himself over the ledge, gripping the metal pipe and began to slide down. Nails screeched in protest as the drain pipe tore loose from the wall. He let go and dropped the last ten feet, turning his ankle when he hit and rolled on the cobblestones in the narrow alley.

"Aahh!" He grimaced, but ignored the pain and rolled over, springing up. Barely sprained. He was still in the chase. Another dislodged roof tile smashed on the stone barely ten feet from him. His quarry was still just above. Abberline dashed around the building on his nearly silent rubber soles, and stopped on the opposite side, listening. Maybe he could confuse this man.

In the distance a shrill police whistle gave the alarm. Just as he turned his head toward the sound, he heard a slight noise above him. He leaned back to look up. A solid weight hit him in the midsection and knocked him sprawling. His pistol skittered across the stone courtyard. Flat on his back, he couldn't breathe; he couldn't move. The stunning impact to his solar plexus was like a blow he'd once received in a rugby match that paralyzed his diaphragm. He heard someone above him take three or four ragged breaths, then a cape brushed his face as the phantom whipped away into the fog.

The pain and paralysis in his chest slowly subsided, and he began to breathe again. He got to his hands and knees and crawled away, looking for his gun. He found it a few feet away, holstered it and rose, unsteadily, to his feet. Voices of awakened residents in the windows above sent him out into the street before someone lit a lantern. Again he heard the shriek of a police whistle, but couldn't tell from which direction, or how far away.

He walked a few steps, trying to regain his breath, and listened. But he heard nothing. "Lost him!" he gasped aloud. He'd gotten himself fit at the Athletic Club, but to no avail. The club! It was less than a block from here. He jogged toward it, guessing that was the direction The Ripper was still headed. He looked between buildings as he went, in hopes the man had passed out from loss of blood, but no luck. He'd duck into the club that was open all night and get a lantern, maybe pick up any constable who might be there.

The back door of the club was standing open, the frame smashed. Abberline tensed, gingerly pushing open the door. He heard the shiver and tinkle of smashing glass and leapt inside, Adams in hand. A cabinet full of vials and jars of lotions and salves had just hit the floor, splattering its contents.

A woman screamed, but it was cut short by a blow. Abberline ran toward the light of a lantern he saw bobbing in the next room. The Ripper, pale as death, had flung off his cape and was holding a bloody towel to his midsection that was covered with blood. Janelle Stafford lay on the floor. "Get back, inspector!" she cried.

Abberline fired, the thunder of the .44 deafening in the room. But the man was too quick and dropped behind a heavy table.

Janelle sprang up and cowered behind Abberline.

From in back of the table came a horrible, wild animal cry, a cross between some jungle cat and a screech, full of pain and fury.

Hair prickled on the back of Abberline's neck. But the cry was followed by the lantern, flung end over end. Abberline barely had time to yank Janelle out of the way as the lantern hit the floor, sliding until it smashed against the wall, spattering burning coal oil. The whole room lit up with flames crackling and licking up the wall toward the ceiling.

The man hurled a chair through a window behind him and leapt through the opening.

"Janelle, ring the fire bell, and keep ringing it until someone comes. I have to go after him."

The last thing Abberline heard as he vaulted through the broken window pane and dashed away was the clanging of the big brass bell, waking the neighborhood and hopefully, bringing the fire brigade and police.

He'd seen with his own eyes that The Ripper was severely wounded and losing blood. He had to slow down soon. There was no way he could keep up this pace.

A noise drew his attention upward. The man had taken to the rooftops again. Abberline had to stay close on his trail or this monster could disappear through a window or roof opening into one of those buildings and lose any pursuit.

Following the sound of footsteps, he ducked into an alley and found an iron fire escape. Up he went, his lungs beginning to labor. He could taste the sulfurous coal smoke in the back of his throat. And his thighs were burning. How could that wounded man keep going?

He reached the top of the second story and caught a glimpse of his quarry leaping across to the next building. He'd shed his cape in the athletic club, and was now unencumbered. The man was an amazing athlete. Abberline thought of himself as fit as he'd been in twenty years, was wearing his rubber-soled canvas athletic shoes and could barely keep up with this man who was leaking out his life's blood from a .44 caliber wound in the midsection. If he hadn't seen the amount of blood by lantern light in the club, he'd have trouble believing the man was even wounded, from the way he was moving. This had to be some kind of bad dream.

Abberline got a run, his soles gripping the edge of the roof as he sprang across a ten-foot gap to the next building. The roof had a slight pitch, but he managed to land on hands and knees, scrabbling for a hold to keep from sliding back. By the time he got to his feet, with skinned knees and hands, he heard the Ripper sliding scrabbling down the other side. To keep his Adams from falling out of its holster again, he jammed it under his belt. He'd fired one shot, so still had four more. But The Ripper had no gun at all, or he would have used it by now to stop his tenacious pursuer.

Gasping, he straddled the ridgepole of the roof, thinking it was no wonder The Ripper had managed to elude capture for so long. Abberline had read stories of the amazing endurance of Australian aborigines, African Zulus and some western American Indian tribes. Some of them could run fifty miles in a day and fight a battle at the end of it. Civilization had robbed city dwellers of this capability. Breath whistling through his teeth, he began to wonder if Jack the Ripper was one of these aborigines. It couldn't be. He'd gotten a clear view of the man in the lantern light at the club.

He slid down the roof, gained momentum and leapt across to the next roof, barely missing a chimney in the fog.

Below in the streets, he heard the clattering of heavy, shod horses and a hand claxon ripping through the fog as the fire wagons headed toward the athletic club. Another police whistle shrieked and Abberline hoped the constables were signaling each other, their warnings leaping ahead of even this madman with superhuman powers. But they couldn't see him in the fog. Abberline knew this would be his one and only chance of catching this killer. If he lost him now, the man might crawl off somewhere and die, or disappear and be hidden by friends, so, if he died, no one would know.

He leapt across to another roof. But he'd lost some of his spring and nearly didn't make the ten-foot jump. He slipped back, clawing at the wooden shakes that came loose under his weight, and managed to catch a foot in the rain gutter to prevent going over the edge. His heart pounding in his chest, he struggled back up to the roof, got to his hands and feet and catwalked up the slope, grabbing a chimney. Coal smoke was billowing out the top into his face and nearly choked him before he could get past it to the windward side.

The Ripper was making no attempt at silence, apparently depending on the fog to hide him. But, this time of the morning, the neighborhood was quiet as the noise of the fire wagons faded behind them. He could still hear the fleeing man scrambling over the rooftops ahead.

Abberline paused at the edge of the roof, wheezing, his lungs trying to process what oxygen there was in the thick atmosphere. Only then did he realize he could no longer hear his quarry. Had he stopped, or gone down to street level? Was he waiting in ambush behind one of the many chimneys that thrust up on the row of brick houses ahead?

Most of the roofs had been nearly level with one another, but through a slight rift in the fog, he sensed the next house was only a single story. Staring off into a fog-filled canyon of space, he knew he'd have to descend to street level. How had Jack crossed this gap? Then he heard his quarry still moving on the rooftops; the sound was receding ahead of him. The gable's pitch on the one-story building was steep. But his blood was up and the chase was on. He'd try it, even if he broke a leg or crashed through into somebody's attic. Getting a running start, he launched himself across to try for the highest point of the opposite roof.

As soon as he struck, he knew he'd made a mistake. The roof

was covered with slate, and the tiles were damp. Even his rubber-soled shoes couldn't grip on the steep, wet surface. He began to slide toward the edge, clawing for purchase with hands, elbows, fingers, knees, feet. Nothing helped. There were no gutters to snag, and off he went, but the drop was only about ten feet to the hard pavement. He flexed his knees and rolled, taking up most of the shock. Bouncing to his feet, he started running, hoping to get ahead of The Ripper.

But the man had changed course and was down off the rooftops, running toward the waterfront, a half-mile distant.

"He'll never make it. He's hit too bad," Abberline grunted aloud as he sprinted along the narrow street. But, amazingly, The Ripper didn't slow down. He'd descended to street level once more and Abberline caught a glimpse of him more than a block ahead running past a street light.

It was like chasing someone in a dream. This wounded phantom of flesh and blood was leaking badly. Even if the man was on some kind of drug, he couldn't keep going. This must be a last ditch effort to reach the river where he had a boat waiting for his escape. Was he a butcher from one of the cattle boats after all? Did he have an accomplice in a steam launch?

In spite of the cool fog, Abberline was soaked with sweat and condensation. His lungs were on fire, but he had to make a supreme effort to stop this man before he reached the river. Yet no amount of extra exertion could close the gap. Where were all the constables? He pulled his Adams and fired twice in the general direction of his unseen quarry. With little hope of hitting him, he thought at least to attract the notice of some nearby constable on the beat.

The damp smell of the river smote his nostrils through the fog. Jack wasn't human. He had to be made of India rubber and piano wire.

Yet, unaccountably, the distance between them finally began to lessen. Abberline closed to within eighty yards, then sixty, then thirty. As the slowing man passed a gaslight near a stone pier, he glanced back over his shoulder, his face ghastly pale in the lamplight.

Now I've got him, Abberline thought. "Halt!" he gasped, too winded to shout.

But The Ripper dashed straight down the length of the stone pier. With a chilling shriek, he threw himself head first into the Thames.

CHAPTER 18

Abberline staggered to a spraddle-legged halt, totally spent. His legs could hardly hold him up. A cold hand seemed to clutch his heart.

"What's going on here?" a uniformed constable yelled, running up, nightstick in hand.

"Inspector Abberline, Scotland Yard," Abberline just managed to gasp, leaning over, hands on knees.

A night watchman appeared from behind a stack of freight on the wharf.

"A man...I was chasing...went in...the river." Abberline was still laboring mightily for breath.

The watchman and the constable ran to the end of the pier, the watchman swinging his lantern.

Abberline walked up to join them. The swirling black water below showed no sign of anyone. He'd either gone down to death, or was swimming underwater beyond the light and making for the other side of the river and safety.

Logic told him the man was dead. But, given what he'd witnessed this night, anything was possible.

"Hal!" the watchman yelled. "Free up that yawl by the stern there!"

"Who's in the water?" The constable looked at Abberline, who was bent over, chest heaving.

"Jack the Ripper."

"Really?" The constable cut his eyes toward the river again.

"He's been shot in the abdomen," Abberline said, straightening up and wiping the moisture from his face with a sleeve. The gray sweater came away streaked with black coal soot.

"He won't be coming up from that current," the constable said.

"Don't underestimate him," Abberline said, beginning to catch his breath. "He just led me on one hell of a chase."

"Maybe the wound wasn't as bad as you thought."

"Worse. Massive bleeding. His strength...nearly inhuman."

"If he comes up, we'll find him, inspector." The night watchman leapt nimbly into the yawl. "Pull around to the sides of the big boats," the watchman said, holding up his lantern.

The constable aided by shining his bullseye lantern on the muddy surface until the yawl was out of range. The boatmen worked their way back and forth among the larger moored vessels, flashing the light over the water. Then Hal rowed out into the current and they began drifting downstream.

Abberline and the policeman paced along the waterfront around stacks of boxes and barrels of freight, watching the lantern growing dimmer in the fog as the yawl moved away.

With each passing minute, Abberline began to think this was a hopeless quest. The world had seen the last of the man who called himself Jack the Ripper. Yet...that wild scream as the man leapt off the pier—a last burst of dying energy? Or...a defiant shout of unfailing strength?

Whatever, or whoever, this man was, he seemed to operate well beyond human limits.

"Unless he's hanging onto something in all this mass of boats, there's only a slim chance he's alive, Inspector," the constable finally said. "I'm a strong swimmer m'self. That current is cold and running faster than a man can jog. A severely wounded man wouldn't last more than five or ten minutes."

"Yes." As Abberline cooled down, he shivered in his damp clothes. To give himself something to do while he waited, he drew his Adams, punched out the three empty shells and reloaded.

Twenty minutes later, the yawl pulled back to the pier. "No sign of him, inspector. Went down and didn't come up. The water's cold. Likely the current will sweep him right out to sea."

Abberline knew the watchman spoke from experience. "Thanks for your help."

"Sorry we didn't get him."

"Constable, can you find a cab? I don't relish walking back to the Three Bells."

"Right away, sir, if there's one anywhere around at this hour." His whistle shrieked in the murky night.

4:55 a.m.
Three Bells Public House

"Inspector!" Annie jumped from her chair and threw her arms around a disheveled, wet Abberline. "Thank God you're safe. Did you catch him?"

"No." Abberline slumped wearily into a chair.

"He got away?" She looked up with alarm.

"You did your part by luring him in and shooting him, but then I couldn't run him down." This last fact still bewildered him. "He jumped into the Thames. I think he's dead, but I can't be sure."

Annie sat back down at the same table and Constable Carrington and the bartender were working on her. For the first time Abberline noticed she was injured.

The bartender soaked a cloth with raw whiskey. She grimaced as he resumed swabbing the cuts and abrasions on her neck.

Abberline picked up the splintered wooden collar that lay on the table. "The Ripper did this?"

"Must've had a grip like a gorilla," Constable Carrington said. "But this collar saved her windpipe from being crushed."

"How do you feel?" Abberline asked, with a twinge of guilt for allowing her to be hurt.

"When I swallow, it feels like something's caught in my

174

throat. Just bruised, I suppose. I'll be okay." She pushed her chair back to show the wide slash in the padded corset. "This kept me in one piece, too."

Abberline shivered at the sight, seeing her bare skin show through in three places. It'd been a very near thing. "You kept your head and did what you set out to do."

"You look like you had a hard time," she said.

He glanced at his streaked image in the back bar mirror. "Oh, just coal soot from a chimney. Jack was running across rooftops a good bit of the way. The closest I got to him was when he jumped off a roof and hit me in the chest with his feet." He rubbed a hand across his bruised sternum. His ankle was also swollen and stiff, but he didn't mention that or his various contusions. His aches and pains were being smothered by the satisfaction that he and Annie Oakley had rid London of Jack the Ripper. "Thank you," he said, breaking into a smile for the first time in a long time.

"You're welcome. I felt I owed it to the women of this city."

"I'm willing to take whatever verbal abuse your husband or Colonel Cody will heap on me," Abberline said. And he meant it.

Beth Hampton returned to the pub at 5:30 and she and Annie fell on each other's necks with exclamations of excitement and relief.

Before Abberline escorted Annie back to the Metropole Hotel, he ordered the bartender to lock the door and cook up a hot breakfast of scrambled eggs, bacon and toast for Constable Carrington, Annie, Beth and himself. While the rising sun was making a valiant effort at burning off the fog, he enjoyed himself as he hadn't in years, by saying nothing, eating, and contemplating the successful outcome of this long nightmare.

The women talked, and Annie filled in her friend with the lurid, horrifying details of her encounter. Beth was wide-eyed. "Then he didn't look anything like that vision I had of him when I was drinking absinthe," she said.

"No. In fact, he was rather average looking. He would never

stand out in a crowd," Annie said. "Except for one thing—his eyes. I will never forget those eyes. When I fired the second time, I saw his eyes in the muzzle flash, less than two feet from my face. I can't describe what they were like." She gave a shudder, and set down her teacup with a trembling hand. "It was like getting a glimpse into the depths of hell."

After breakfast, Abberline called the barman and Beth Hampton aside and bought their silence with twenty pounds each. "You can tell your grandchildren the truth of what happened," Abberline said.

"Thank you, inspector," Beth managed to gasp, clutching the crisp notes in disbelief, her fair cheeks flushing. "With this I can rent a decent place to live and maybe find a regular job."

A combination of the rising sun and a slight westerly breeze had eliminated most of the fog by the time Abberline and Annie caught a Hansom back to the Metropole.

"Let me break the news to them," Annie said when they were rolling toward her hotel.

"All right. I'll back you up."

"Are you serious about keeping my name out of this, once the news hits the papers?"

"If you wish, I'll do all I can to make sure you are only the anonymous heroine who helped Scotland Yard rid Whitechapel of Jack the Ripper."

"Then we might have a leak right here." She reached inside her blouse and extracted a big knife.

"Where did you get that?"

"Constable Carrington found it where I was attacked." She turned over the heavy blade. "It's an American Bowie knife, named for the inventor, Jim Bowie, the frontiersman who was killed at the Alamo, over fifty years ago."

"I've seen pictures of them," Abberlline said, testing the edge with his thumb.

"That's' a common enough knife in America," she said, "but that's not the original handle. Appears to be a piece of elkhorn. It's an Indian knife. Don't know what tribe, but see those tiny arrows and the stick figure of a deer incised into the handle?"

"Good heft and balance," Abberline said.

"I've gone over that attack in my mind constantly since it happened a few hours ago," she continued. "Just as he was trying to rip open my stomach, something whistled past my ear and I heard him gasp. Then it clattered to the pavement. Carrington even showed me traces of blood on the blade." She pointed to the groove in the heavy blade. "Somebody threw that knife and hit The Ripper, but it didn't stick. Must have been a glancing blow."

Abberline looked at her expectantly. "You know whose this is?"

She nodded. "I think so."

"An Indian with the show?"

"Yes. A young Sioux who's a friend of Matt Vickers, my 'gun boy'."

"Then someone besides me and Constable Carrington were there keeping an eye on you."

"Apparently."

"Did you tell anyone else about our arrangement? Besides your husband and Colonel Cody?"

"No. But Matt is in and out of our tent constantly. He could have overheard something."

Abberline nodded. "Very difficult to keep a secret like this from leaking out."

She looked at the knife again. "But I thought both those boys left on the train a few days ago when the show packed up and started for Southampton."

"If Cody can find them, tell him I'll have a little reward for them if they keep quiet about this and their part in it." With the threat of exposure, Abberline's sense of satisfaction was beginning to ebb. Annie was an overwhelming favorite of the British public, but would Scotland Yard be ridiculed for having to recruit an American female marksman to do their most important job for them? He cringed at the thought of what the newspapers would say. Yet, his idea, sparked by Sir Charles Warren, *had* rid society of Jack the Ripper. Or had it? There was no hard evidence he was dead, and a strong doubt lingered in Abberline's mind. With a man this hard to kill, he wanted proof.

Whatever misgivings Abberline had about Frank Butler's and William Cody's reaction to Annie's minor injuries were swept away when Annie broke the news to them. Frank hugged his wife and shook Abberline's hand, expressing great relief it was over.

Cody broke out a bottle of his best aged bourbon and insisted they all have a drink to celebrate, even though it was only 8:15 in the morning.

"Frank, someone threw this knife out of the fog when I was being attacked. I think it wounded The Ripper. Do you recognize it?"

"That belongs to Crowfoot, Matt's friend," Frank said, without hesitation. "I tried to trade him out of it a time or two, but he wouldn't give it up."

"That Indian boy stayed behind?" Cody sipped his drink and smoothed his mustache.

"I'd guess both he and Matt are somewhere in London," Frank said. "Those two are inseparable. Somehow they found out about this."

"They likely thought it was some great adventure to get in on the plot and the action," Cody said. "Can't say as I blame them. I would've done the same when I was their age."

"Well, if they don't miss the ship back to America, I'll have a few words with them when I return this knife," Frank Butler said.

"Go easy on them," Abberline said. "Just be sure you extract a promise of silence."

"If they were actually there, and he threw this knife, that'll be tough to do," Cody surmised. "I'd be bustin' to tell everybody I knew, or be selling my story to *THE POLICE GAZETTE.*"

"Well, a few weeks from now, it probably won't really matter," Abberline said. "Other crises and scandals will hit the papers. The Ripper will be history."

CHAPTER 19

Three Days Later

"We're almighty lucky," Doctor Llewellyn said as he stepped outside the autopsy room with Abberline. The late November wind was sweeping across the cobblestone courtyard beside the City of London Hospital. "The cold water has preserved the body to a remarkable degree."

"Lucky to have a body at all," Abberline added, breathing deeply of the cold, clean air that was blowing down from the north. The biting wind was preferable to the stifling odor of formaldehyde and urine inside.

"Snagged on brush in a bend of the river not three miles downstream," the doctor said.

"And found by a fisherman," Abberline finished. "Well, it may be luck, but we deserve a bit of luck, as hard as we've all worked on this case."

"It has certainly provided the newspapers with plenty of material."

Abberline nodded. "Now with the body being discovered, there will be a lot more from the papers. They're all clamoring to know his identity."

"That's still up in the air," the doctor said. "The word is out in the district for anyone who wishes to come and look at him before the autopsy starts to see if they can identify him. The body is being kept on ice."

"What about his fingerprints?" Abberline asked.

Doctor Llewellyn shook his head. "Surgeon Brown and I thought about that, but the skin has deteriorated just enough that no fingerprints can be obtained."

"Wouldn't really matter, anyway," Abberline said. "That science is so new, Scotland Yard and the London Police haven't built up a base file of criminal fingerprints to compare them to. So, identifying him that way would be a very long shot, indeed, unless he has an extensive criminal record and has been fingerprinted before. I suppose it was too much to expect that he'd have something in his pockets to tell us who he is. Even his cape burned up in the fire at the Police Athletic Club."

"Part of a watch chain was hanging from a buttonhole in his vest, but the watch must have been lost in the river. You want to take a look at him?"

"I saw him when they brought him in," Abberline said. "How have you preserved him?"

"Packed in ice in a metal box, with his face showing through a glass like a coffin."

"Let's hope someone knows who he is," the doctor said. "The official photographer has made several exposures of his face and his body, so the pictures will be on file, in case someone comes along later who knows him. But I'll lay odds he'll be recognized by someone in the Whitechapel district."

"I'd hate for his true identity to remain anonymous for all time," Abberline said. "Will his body go to a pauper's grave?"

"London Hospital has requested his brain for study."

"Think they'll find anything unusual?"

Llewellyn shrugged. "It's worth a try, I guess. If there's some deformity or chemical imbalance, it might account for his vicious, bizarre behavior. If not, the cause could be hidden deeper inside the brain cells. Or…the result of undetectable phobia, lust, a violent fixation on whores from something in his past. Who knows? Brains of geniuses and madmen have been studied before and revealed no variant from an average, normal brain."

"Something more spiritual than physical," Abberline concurred.

"As to his body, I've heard talk among the medical students that it should be preserved in alcohol and sold to the highest bidder as a curiosity, and the money distributed to the poor prostitutes in the East End."

"A bit of poetic justice."

"Yes. There aren't many cases of actual justice in this Vale of Tears."

"The body on display…a modern equivalent of a criminal's head being stuck on a pike at the city gates," Abberline said. "We haven't progressed very far from the time of Cromwell."

The doctor pulled up his overcoat collar. "Let's go inside. I'm about to freeze in this wind."

Doctor Llewellyn was right. At three that afternoon, after a steady stream of men and women had filed through the open door of an anteroom to view the remains, a woman named Martha Kimball, landlady of a lodging house on Goulston Street, said the dead man was Archer Preston, a boarder at her house whom she hadn't seen in the past four days.

Mrs. Kimball, a widow, had a stricken look on her long, pale face as she faced Abberline and Dr. Llewellyn in a private office at the hospital. "I didn't want to force the lock on his door until I was sure he wasn't coming back," she said, wringing a handkerchief in her hands. "But that's him, all right. I'm sure of it. I can't believe he's Jack the Ripper. He was kind and considerate to me. Always paid his rent on time. Oh my! The reputation of my place is ruined," she wailed softly. "To think that I housed Jack the Ripper under my roof!"

"It's no fault of yours, Mrs. Kimball. But we do need to see his room. I'll get Constable Carrington, and the three of us, along with Doctor Brown, will come straightaway."

Mrs. Kimball opened the second floor room with her passkey and led the way inside. A foul, musty odor, and the smell of rotting meat washed over them.

"Oh, my!" she exclaimed. "He must have let some food spoil in here."

Abberline sniffed, and his stomach nearly rebelled. "Open that window, Carrington."

Even with the window up and a slight, cold breeze moving the curtain, the stench was nearly overpowering.

Doctor Llewellyn pulled back a drape hanging at the end of the iron bedstead. "Ho! What's this?"

A tiny bedside table covered with a black cloth supported a human skull. On either side were two thick candles in brass holders.

The four men crowded around the table.

"An altar," Abberline said. "Facing north." A geometric symbol he recognized as a pentagram, was painted on the black altar cloth. A more powerful odor came from underneath the altar, and Abberline bent down for a closer look. "Some kind of rotting meat," he said. pulling out a bowl.

"Hard to tell, but appears to be a piece of kidney," Doctor Llewellyn said. "Maybe the part he didn't eat or send you in the post."

Doctor Brown slid back the fancy grillwork from the coal grate. "More in here. Didn't all burn." He took a poker and raked it out. "Looks like the remains of a liver."

"Oh, this is frightful!" Mrs. Kimball said, standing in the open doorway.

"Where do you suppose he got the skull?" Carrington asked.

"Maybe from one of his earlier victims," Abberline said. "Or, he could have robbed a grave or even stolen it from a medical school. The important thing is, he apparently was practicing devil worship."

"Well, I know very little about the occult," Doctor Brown said.

"Nor do I," Abberline said. "We'll call in an expert on the subject. But, from all appearances, he was offering sacrifice of human organs. We'll seal this room off and have it examined, inch by inch."

"Did you have any indication this was going on, Mrs. Kimball?" Carrington asked.

"Oh, no!" She seemed horrified by the idea. "I knew he liked to cook some of his own meals up here. I didn't object. It allowed him to save a few shillings, you know. But I was constantly warning him about the danger of fire outside the grate. And, all the time, he was really cooking and eating parts of human bodies of women he'd killed. And worshipping the Prince of Darkness to boot."

For a few seconds, Abberline thought the old lady was going to faint, and he moved quickly to her side. He helped her to the only seat—a straight-backed wooden chair.

The men spent another ten minutes examining the room, but found nothing but a few garbled notes scribbled on sheets of paper in the table drawer. There was even a prayer to Satan. Abberline took some of these as handwriting samples.

They found no knives in the room. Abberline half expected the man had more than one, but apparently the long, sharp blade he used to slit throats and disembowel his victims had gone into the river with him and not been recovered.

Abberline questioned Mrs. Kimball about the man's habits, and asked if several names written on a slip of paper were names of other men, or aliases. The names were not familiar to her.

It was after six when the two doctors, the constable and Abberline left the lodging house after cautioning Mrs. Kimball to say nothing to anyone else about this until the investigation was complete.

"What's next?" Abberline asked Doctor Llewellyn as the four men went downstairs to the street.

"Doctor Brown and I will perform the autopsy first thing in

the morning. You're welcome to come watch if you like."

"Thanks. I might pop in and out. Strong drink and post mortems are two things my stomach doesn't handle well before noon."

The doctor chuckled.

"You know, Annie's heart and uterus could have been next on that sacrificial altar," Abberline said as they stepped out into the November dusk.

CHAPTER 20

Next morning, while the autopsy was underway, Abberline stopped by his office to compare the handwriting samples to the "Dear Boss" letter. The samples matched.

Buoyed by this finding, he went on to visit Janelle Stafford at her aunt's home. It was an unusually warm, sunny day for late November, and he found her seated at an easel, painting a watercolor in the enclosed courtyard behind the house. She was copying a scene from a travel handbill showing the sun shining on the white cliffs of Dover.

"Ah, inspector. It's wonderful to see you." She rose and extended a slim hand. She looked a bit peaked in the wan sunshine. But, as he took her hand, he realized he'd seen her only in the yellow glow of coal oil lamps at the Police Athletic Club.

"I would've come to check on you earlier, but…"

"I know," she smiled, waving off his apology, "you've been one of the busiest men in London. It's all over the papers." She sat down and patted the stone bench beside her. He sat.

"I haven't been by to look at the club. Is it a total wreck?"

She shook her head as she swished her brush in a vial of water, and wiped it on a cloth. "Not really. The damp fog and lack of wind probably saved it. But it'll take months to repair and rebuild part of it—the back part mainly, where he threw the lantern. It'll be closed down for a good while." She smiled. "You won't have anywhere to work out or play tennis."

"More to the point, you won't have a job."

"I was told I could work part time in an office at the Yard." She made a wry face. "Not sure I could stand that. "I'm not the clerical type."

They chatted for another half hour while her aunt brought them tea and tiny cinnamon buns.

Finally, the sun went under a cloud and a chilly wind sprang up, gusting across the courtyard, turning the sunny day into one reflected by cold gray stones of the enclosing walls. All too soon such pleasant respites were over, and it was back to the hard reality of his job. Some day, he promised himself, he'd take a proper holiday to some warm climate—maybe Jamaica. That had been his dream for years. He wasn't getting any younger. It was time to withdraw his savings and go. The work at the Yard could be done by someone else. He wasn't indispensable. He didn't want to become one of those old codgers whose life was defined by his job.

He pulled out his watch. Doctor Llewellyn would be close to finishing his autopsy. As he slid the watch back into his waistcoat, Janelle, instead of offering her hand, stepped up, slipped her arms around his neck and kissed him lightly on the cheek.

"Well, I won't question the reason for that," he said, taken aback, "but it's the best reward I've had in a long time."

"Thanks for coming to my aid that night," she said. "The Ripper would likely have killed me. At the very least I would have died of fright."

He took her by the shoulders. "Give me a few days to clear up this business, and I'll look in on you again. Get plenty of rest, and do something to keep your mind off The Ripper. He's dead and gone, and will never bother us again."

She smiled. "I have my painting and my books. My aunt and I go shopping." She sighed. "But I'll never get over the sight of those eyes of his." She shivered visibly and pulled her smock close about herself.

Annie had mentioned the same thing. Abberline didn't recall anything particular about the man's eyes. But unlike these women, he hadn't seen them up close with death staring out from them.

"Winter is coming on," he said. "Maybe you need a vacation with your aunt to some sunny place where there is a nice white sand beach, and a place to have dinner and dance."

She laughed with a sound like softly chiming bells. "The very thing I was thinking of. Inspector, you're a mind reader after all. You could probably know what The Ripper was thinking."

"I'm afraid not. If that were the case, I'd have stopped him long before now."

"I suppose you're not going to tell me who this mystery woman was you recruited to bait the killer. The newspapers are speculating about her identity. They've named everyone from Bertie's mistress to your landlady."

"I chose a woman with the musk you told me about. She lured him in, but it apparently wasn't an amorous attraction."

She laughed.

"Maybe someday I'll tell you."

She escorted him out the gate and around to the busy street where he hailed a passing Hansom.

Abberline reached London Hospital ten minutes before Doctor Llewellyn and Doctor Brown finished their post mortem. Abberline held his breath and entered the autopsy room, sliding up behind the cluster of med students, police and selected spectators. Looking between two pairs of shoulders, he could see the pale, naked body stretched out under the glare of the gaslight. He'd never seen a corpse so white. But that was no surprise, considering the amount of blood the man had lost, and his having been in the cold river for nearly three days.

Doctor Llewellyn turned from the table, and Abberline caught his eye, motioning with his head toward the courtyard. The doctor nodded, and the inspector edged back out of the crowd and went outside. It was nearing high noon, but the air was still cold, an overcast having hidden the weak sunshine.

Fifteen minutes later, the doctor came out, rolling down his sleeves. He slipped into his tweed jacket. He seldom wore a hat except to ward off rain or snow, and the fitful breeze ruffled his thick gray hair. "Let's walk," he said, striding ahead.

Abberline fell in beside him as they started toward Turner Street. The doctor didn't say anything for the first five minutes, as if he were letting the cold wind clear his head. "How about a pint and a bite to eat?" he finally suggested, nodding toward the White Horse pub.

The Inspector followed him inside. It was lunchtime and the place was crowded with a mixture of laborers and office workers, along with employees of the nearby hospital. They sought out a booth, ordering Porter and ham sandwiches, with hot mustard.

"While we were gone to look at The Ripper's room, George Hutchinson came in and identified the body as the man he'd seen and described to you," the doctor said.

"Good. Another confirmation," Abberline said. "Just as I suspected, the man lived close by. He was seen around Whitechapel and nobody gave him a second look; too mild and ordinary looking. Carrington said the man was one of many questioned by the police weeks ago, but they had no reason to hold him, even on suspicion. A regular in the neighborhood. Mrs. Kimball, his landlady, said he'd rented the room six months ago, and she showed me the agreement he signed. According to some of those papers in his drawer, he apparently went by many aliases—Robert Cinatas being one—which happens to be Satanic, spelled backwards. A schoolboy joke. She said he didn't appear to have a job, and kept odd hours, coming and going at all times of day and night. He also called himself Thomas Janklow, Abraham Pottsworth, and Gabriel Sanderson. Unless some relative comes forward, it's not likely we'll know who he actually is—or was."

"And who is going to publicly admit being related to Jack the Ripper?" the doctor asked, sipping the foam from his glass of dark Porter.

"Precisely. That's why the official photographer took several exposures so that if someone turns up later, we have images on file."

"There's no doubt we have the right man, anyway," the

doctor said. "As to the autopsy, it was rather routine, with a couple of exceptions. The cold water preserved the body so it was almost as if the corpse was put on ice at the time of death. We found a .45 bullet that had apparently snapped the gold watch chain in two, deflecting upward, broke a rib, clipped the aorta and lodged near the spine. He had what appeared to be a knife wound in the side of the neck. At least something sharp barely sliced the muscles on the left side.

"Probably a Bowie knife, but I'll fill you in on that later," Abberline said.

"Annie didn't know it, but she got him a second time with one of her last off hand shots. Normally, I'd attribute that hit to luck but, in her case, it had to be skill. Lying on the ground, she anticipated where he was by the sound of his footsteps in the fog, and winged him. Bullet passed completely through the muscle of his upper arm without hitting anything vital. Even if he hadn't already received a mortal wound, that through and through arm injury must have made it very difficult to climb."

"What was the actual cause of death?"

"Water in the lungs indicated he was alive when he hit the river. As far as the exact cause of death, Doctor Brown and I aren't so certain. More than likely, it was due to a combination of factors— shock, hypothermia, suffocation by drowning, and loss of blood." Doctor Llewellyn took a deep breath and stroked his sidewhiskers, pausing for the aproned waiter to set down their two sandwiches.

"Will that be all, gentlemen?"

"Yes, thank you."

The waiter withdrew.

"You were saying?" Abberline prompted.

"There was evidence of massive hemorrhaging."

"I know."

"I went to a map and traced the route you said you chased him," the doctor said. "Many blocks, up and down and across rooftops of buildings, and a long sprint to the river."

"Yes."

"And you actually saw him covered with blood inside the Police Athletic Club."

"That's right."

"This man was somewhat smaller than average size. From the tear in the aorta, he could not have walked a half block, much less done what you said he did."

"Maybe the wound worsened with exertion."

Doctor Llewellyn shook his head. "There's not that much blood in the human body—ten pints in his case. No more. And he would have passed out long before that much drained out. What he did, physically, was humanly impossible."

Abberline stared at his friend. "Then, how do you account for it? I saw him do it."

The doctor sipped his porter, ignoring the sandwich. For several seconds, the pub background noise filled the silence between them.

"I'm a man of science, but I've seen things in my career that defy logic—a man who was thought dead waking up in the morgue, a woman recovering almost overnight from what should have been a mortal disease—and other things of that nature that were beyond any medical explanation. Some would label them miracles."

"Hard to believe God would suspend the laws of nature on The Ripper's behalf."

"I'm not saying it was God."

"The Devil, then?"

"After what we saw in his room earlier, would that theory be too far-fetched?"

"So you think the Devil was responsible?"

"I think Jack the Ripper was actually possessed by the Devil. The Evil One had completely taken over his body and mind, and used supernatural force to perform those feats of endurance."

Abberline sat back in the booth and stared at his practical friend. "You don't mean it?"

"I do mean it. There have been many documented cases of demonic possession—and exorcism—over the centuries. You think,

191

just because we live in the modern, enlightened world of nineteenth century medical science, that such a thing can't happen now?"

"It just seems unlikely."

"Unlikely it may be, but do you have any other explanation?"

"What reason would Satan have for possessing this man?"

The doctor shrugged. "Why does he possess anyone? I don't recall there was any reason given in the Bible for demonic possession of particular individuals. Satan apparently has his own reasons—and his own methods of gathering human souls for his infernal kingdom. Some of my colleagues who don't believe in God or His fallen angels, or even in an afterlife, would deny this and accuse me of unscientific diagnosis or conclusions. But there is no other explanation for that massive blood loss not being quickly fatal. A supernatural being could have kept him going until he reached the river. There have been cases of levitation, of heads turning completely around without breaking the neck, and feats of superhuman strength, such as breaking metal bonds."

"My heavens!" Abberline breathed. "That explains a lot of why he was able to escape so quickly, so often."

"Do you recall the New Testament story of Christ driving the Devils out of a man possessed, and the Devils cried out to Jesus for permission to enter a herd of swine? With His consent, the Devils entered the swine, who immediately went crazy, stampeded down a hill, plunged off a cliff into the sea and drowned."

"I remember that story."

"This time the possessed man plunged into the Thames and drowned."

Abberline swallowed, his appetite suddenly gone. "Don't woo the Devil unless you're serious about winning him."

"That's about the size of it," the doctor said, finally taking a bite of his sandwich. "Doctor Brown and I discussed this, and he's of the same opinion. It had to be something beyond the laws of nature. Demonic possession, triggered by Devil worship and human sacrifice as evidenced by what we saw in his room. Although we can't prove that at an inquest, it's the most likely explanation."

"I wonder what will happen when this story gets out?" Abberline said.

"Why should it? You've done your job and stopped The Ripper. That's all anyone else needs to know."

Abberline pondered this for a moment. "But Her Majesty should be told."

"The Queen can be very discreet."

"You're right."

"When you retire and write your memoirs in the twentieth century, you can reveal our secret to the world," Doctor Llewellyn said. He took a long swallow of his stout as if that put an end to the matter.

CHAPTER 21

"Crowfoot, I don't think I can walk another step." To emphasize his statement, Matt Vickers sat down on the shiny rail, hanging his head between his knees.

"I go leave you then," the young Sioux said, trudging on ahead, along the deserted railroad track.

The sun was high, but the season was late and the warmth of the cheerful orb had fled.

"You just wanta show off that you're an Indian with a lot more endurance."

Crowfoot stopped and turned around. "You can do it. You want to be left behind when ship sails?"

"The ship has probably already left."

"No. Annie and Frank and Cody still in London. Ship won't leave without them."

"But they'll catch a train to Southampton and get there before we can. Even if we could walk all the way to the coast, we'd never get there in time."

"Why we have to walk?"

"You got enough money for two tickets? We got just about enough to buy food, and that's it."

"We sell your knife. Bring in plenty."

"Oh, no you don't. I found this knife and I ain't giving it up. No telling how many throats it's slashed."

"How you prove it belongs to The Ripper?" Crowfoot asked.

"You saw where I found it. I don't know if Annie hit him, but he dropped it right after we heard her last shot. He was only a half block from her. Nobody uses a knife like this except a butcher or a doctor—or a killer," Matt said. "You should have gone after your own knife."

"We no get mixed up in all that. I threw my knife, and hit Jack, but he run off anyway."

"A bad throw in the fog."

"I hit him."

"Well, it didn't kill him."

"Annie best shot in the world, and she didn't kill him—with five shots," the Indian retorted. "Can't pick up my knife because constable there, and carry it off for evidence. Think it belongs to The Ripper."

"Yeah. Best we didn't go running up there to get it. We'd have been held for questioning, if nothing else," Matt conceded. He looked behind them, and then ahead. "We gonna camp out tonight?"

"No food, no water, no blankets. How we camp?"

"We got matches. We can collect some brush for a fire."

"Cold sleeping on ground this time of year."

"Guess we shouldn't have sent our stuff on ahead with the show."

"Had to make it look like we were going, too."

"That's so. But these clothes are getting smelly."

"We washed underwear and buy new shirts," Crowfoot said.

"I reckon it was all worth it if we can get to Southampton before the ship leaves." Matt reached under his shirt and extracted a long knife that was wrapped in his old dirty shirt to keep the edge from his skin. "Just look at this," he said, in awe of the long, slender blade, sharp as a barber's razor. "Kinda gives ya the willies, just to look at it, don't it? Especially knowin' where it's been. Slashing open innards, and cuttin' out kidneys and wombs and things."

The gutta percha handle was ribbed for a better grip, there was no cross guard, as on a dagger and the blade itself was about twelve inches long, an inch wide, with a slightly rounded tip—an instrument meant for slicing, not for stabbing or puncturing.

"I've seen knives like this in a museum," Matt declared, holding it up for inspection. "In a surgeon's kit from the Civil War. It was in a wooden box lined with green velvet. The kit had a saw for cutting off arms and legs. There was some other stuff in there, too, that I didn't know nothing about."

"You talk too much about blood and death," Crowfoot said.

"Blood and death might be what we can make money on," Matt said, "if we can sell our story to a magazine or newspaper back home. You saw those papers in London; readers love this kinda stuff."

"You write story in good English, and tell about my Bowie knife," Crowfoot said. "Tell how I wounded The Ripper. Then you take picture of that doctor's knife you have." He shook his head. "But nobody believe us and not pay for story until they ask Cody and Annie. And they don't know. Best we keep quiet or get into big trouble." He turned and started walking again.

"You give up too easy, Crofe," Matt said, jumping up and hurrying after him. "We'll have to come out in public, for sure, but we can do that. We'll be famous. People will want our autograph, like they do Annie's."

"Then we must tell that Annie trapped Ripper." The Indian stopped and turned to him. "You say you hear Annie and Frank talk. They not want anyone else to know Annie was bait for The Ripper. Cody fire us if we do this."

"Yeah, I guess there's no way we could go public and keep Annie's privacy," Matt agreed.

They walked along the ties in silence.

"If the constable shows Annie that Bowie, she'll know it's yours," Matt finally said. "What then?"

"She be mad as hell."

"Maybe she'll pay us to keep quiet."

"Whites call that blackmail."

"You're right."

"She might tell Cody to fire us if we talk," Crowfoot said.

"Damn! We got a great story here and we can't tell it," Matt said, waving the long, slender knife around over his head. He leapt to one side and slashed at the air like a duelist, the edge whistling through the air. The sun flashed off the polished steel. "Too bad there's no blood on this," he said, examining it more closely.

"If it had blood, it would be Annie's," the Indian said, "unless Ripper not wash it since last time."

"You got a point."

They continued walking.

"Wish it was summer. Then I wouldn't care how long it took us to get to the coast." He glanced around at the brown grass in the meadows flanking the right-of-way. "You think Annie, Frank and Cody will leave for Southampton right away?" Matt asked.

"Maybe today. Maybe tomorrow. Cost Cody much money every day the show waits."

"Hadn't thought of that. Cody's a generous man, but Nate Salsbury won't let him waste money like that. Well, that means we have to get there no later than they do, or we'll be left behind. They won't wait for us."

"If Annie has my Bowie, she knows we were there. Maybe they send someone to look for us."

"And maybe they won't. We're old enough to take care of ourselves, and we could be anywhere in London."

Matt wrapped the long knife in his old shirt and stowed it inside his clothes, next to his skin. "Like I said before, I ain't walking all these miles to Southampton, miss the ship and then have to try to get a job in England over the winter just to survive. I'm for getting to the port and getting on that ship before it pulls out."

"How you do that?"

"We're walking on these train tracks, aren't we? See how shiny these rails are? We're on the main line. Next train that comes, we figure a way to get aboard. Anybody catches us, we tell 'em we're broke and you're from India and we gotta got to Southampton to get a ship to work your way back home. Robber took all our money and can we please ride free in the baggage car."

Crowfoot snorted his contempt at the idea. "They no give us free ride. This is England. Only tramps in big cities can beg and get things."

"Maybe a freight will come along instead of a highballing passenger express."

"How we stop it? Go too fast."

"I got more experience than you when it comes to hopping freights." He looked around. "We're on a long stretch between towns so they'll be barreling along here. We gotta find a tight curve or a steep grade or a water tower where the locomotive will slow down or stop. But it can't be at a depot. Let's hustle up and find such a place, before another train comes along." He broke into a jog.

"I thought you tired."

"Got my second wind."

"Crofe! Wake up."

The Indian stirred out of the nest he'd made in the dry grass along the cutbank, out of the wind. The sun had disappeared and dusk was settling in.

"Listen."

A long, mournful whistle sounded in the distance.

"Blowing for that crossing about a mile back," Matt said. "Let's hope they need water from this tower. Back in the states, locomotives stop at nearly every tank. Those steamers use lots of water."

Two minutes later, they heard a chuffing and a green locomotive rolled around a long curve and began to slow.

"She's stopping," Matt said. "Be ready. It's coming on to dark. Watch for the conductor or brakeman with a lantern, and keep clear of him. I ain't familiar with British trains, but they gotta be pretty much the same as ours."

The big engine with seven-foot, hooded drive wheels ground to a halt in a blast of steam several rods beyond them.

"Looks like a mix of three passenger coaches and three

freight."

A single trainman was walking along beside the train, swinging a shuttered lantern.

"Follow me," Matt whispered. The Indian melted in behind him and the pair crept toward the end of the train. A clatter and the rush of water as the big spout was swung into place over the engine and the boiler took on water. Matt was counting on the noise and activity at the head of the train to divert attention from the darkened rear. He crept up to the side of the train. Both of them were wearing dark shirts and pants. He searched quickly along the side for an open door, but all the freight cars were closed and locked. He looked frantically. They had only a few minutes. Keeping an eye out for the brakeman, he rolled under the high cars and scanned the opposite side. Apparently all the freight cars were full and closed.

There was a clatter as the counterbalanced spout was swung back up into place against the water tower. Matt saw the flash of the brakeman's lantern, on the opposite side of the train as he signaled the engineer. It was now or never. He waited until the train jerked into motion, and saw the brakeman's legs as he stepped up on the end platform of the last car.

"Now!" He led the way and the two of them dashed for the steps and platform between two of the three locked freight cars. They grabbed the handrails and hopped aboard before the train had time to gather speed.

"We won't be seen here while we're moving," Matt said over the banging of the coupling beneath. "But we'll have to stay here for hours. We just have to be ready to dodge if we come into a lighted depot, or stop at another water tower."

"How far?" Crowfoot asked.

"Just an overnight run when we came up to London back in the Spring. If we can hold down this rattler, we'll be in Southampton by daylight."

CHAPTER 22

March 21, 1889
Nutley, New Jersey

Annie Oakley struggled to escape. But she was held down. She kicked and fought, tried to scream, but a shadowy figure gripped her throat, choking off any sound.

With a mighty lunge, she finally broke through the surface of consciousness, and found herself entangled in the sheets. Heart pounding, and moist with perspiration, she sat up in bed. The nightmare receded, and her breathing began to slow.

Husband Frank still slept, so she slipped out of bed and padded softly out of the dark bedroom, closing the door behind her.

In the kitchen she reached above the stove for a match, struck it, lifted the glass chimney and lighted the coal oil lamp. By its reassuring glow, she saw things were still in their proper place. She carried the lamp into the living room, disdaining to put on a robe in the chilly house. The cool air felt good after the suffocating nightmare. She sat down in her favorite armchair, tucking her bare feet up under her.

The pendulum in the mantel clock counted the seconds with a steady ticking. The hands pointed at 5:40.

How long would she have to endure this recurring nightmare? Actually, two nightmares. In one, a dark figure was choking her, pinning her down so she couldn't move her arms or legs. Sometimes, her attacker was slashing at her abdomen. Then, a flash of light revealed his eyes—a sight so terrifying she thought she'd seen the Devil, himself.

In the other variation of the nightmare, she pulled the trigger of her Merwin Hulbert and the explosion blew the shadowy figure off her and he went staggering away in the fog, screaming that he was shot and dying. She held her pistol, while waves of guilt washed over her. She'd killed another human, and could do nothing to reverse her action.

Maybe she should seek professional help. But she instinctively knew that time would be the only remedy for this ailment of the mind. It had taken years for her to stop having bad dreams about being abused as a slave to "The Wolves". This episode with Jack the Ripper had lasted only a few minutes, from beginning to end. Surely, her memory of it would soon fade. After all, it had been only four months since it happened. In her conscious hours, she often replayed the sequence, from the time Abberline had come to request her help, to the time he'd returned to the Three Bells pub and told her The Ripper had leapt into the river. Logically, she knew she had done the right thing. She'd used her bravery and skill to rid the world of a maniac who was committing vicious murders. Surely, God would not harshly judge him because he was mad, not in possession of his own free will. She'd received a letter only a week before from Chief Inspector Frederick Abberline confiding to her that he and the doctors who'd performed the autopsy had come to the conclusion that Jack the Ripper, whose identity was still a mystery, was actually possessed by the Devil. And certainly a man who had no control over his own actions could not be held responsible for them. Her killing of him was like shooting a rabid mountain lion, she reasoned.

She got up and went to the chest in the corner where she kept her many shooting medals. Opening the lid, she picked out a circular gold medal twice as large as a silver dollar. It was suspended from a silk ribbon that bore the colors of the British Union Jack. With it was an envelope bearing the seal of the British Royal family. She removed the letter she'd read many times and looked at it again.

In part, it read, "…because of various restrictions, procedures and to protect your privacy, we are unable to award you the Victoria Cross, our highest decoration for valor against the enemy. The VC, in any event, is intended to be a military award. Instead, we have ordered a one-of-a-kind medal struck and inscribed. I hope you will wear it with pride in future years…" The letter was signed by Queen Victoria. Beneath the printed letter and her official signature and titles, the queen had appended a personal postscript in her own hand, "It required a woman to save us." Annie smiled as she turned over the medal and saw the profile of the diminutive monarch. On the reverse, it was engraved, *To Annie Oakley, in remembrance of her magnificent courage and skill in saving London from Jack the Ripper, the people of London and the British Empire award this emblem of their profoundest gratitude.* The queen's signature was replicated in the soft gold, along with the date, November, 1888.

Annie clutched the medallion in her hand, feeling its warmth. It had been worth it, after all, she decided, yet again. Abusers and killers had to be stopped. This was a flawed world, and it was up to people like her, Inspector Abberline and all law enforcement officers to keep some semblance of order.

She returned the medal and the letter to the chest, closed it and turned the key in the lock. The matter was over and done with. Today was the first day of Spring, and it was time to turn her attention to the upcoming season with the Wild West Show. Time to let go of the past. Bill Cody had fired Lillian Smith, the chunky teenage sharpshooter from California. This eliminated the bone of contention that nearly caused Annie and Frank to quit the show. This year of 1889 was going to be bigger and better. Bill Cody and Nate Salsbury had planned a grand European tour that included, not only England again, but also France, Belgium, Germany, Spain and Italy. It would be a very full season.

She went into the kitchen to fire up the cookstove and brew a pot of coffee before Frank got up. They would sell this house and she could be rid of her aggravating domestic chores, including the necessity of hiring and firing cooks and housekeepers.

She and Frank would be on the road again, and she could
hardly wait.

CHAPTER 23

The Midlands
June, 1905

"Blimey, Ned, we can't be giving up our meal ticket!"

Tall, lean Ned Ashworth put an arm around his partner, Terry Collins, and walked him away from the tent where the body of Jack the Ripper was on display. "There comes a time, Terrence, m'boy, to let go and move on."

"Move on to what?" Collins took off his soft cap and rubbed a hand across his bald pate. The fringe of hair circling his head was ruffed up, badly in need of a trim. He blinked in the bright sunlight. "Why didn't you ask me before you started talking about selling out? After all, we been partners, now, for twelve years."

"Thirteen years, but that's not the issue," Ashworth said, removing a cigar stub from the corner of his mouth. "Look at it this way. It's been a good run, but our time is done. We need to get back to what we do best—stage acting and legerdemain. That's our natural calling."

"But we have a new generation paying to look at the most famous criminal in English history. Why sell him?"

"You haven't been paying attention to the details. Our receipts have slacked off the last six months, and even in the summer they haven't picked back up. We've displayed the body all over England, Wales and Scotland. Everybody who has any interest in seeing him have already come and paid and gawked—many of them more than once. We've used up the market. The younger folk don't care anythin' about history, and The Ripper is definitely history now."

"But he has a few good years left, Collins persisted. "At least one or two more seasons at the county fairs."

"We've had to do some repairs to keep him from coming apart. All this travelin' has been 'ard on him," Ned said. He held up a hand as Collins started to object. "Figure it this way…how long would it take us to collect five hundred pounds on admission fees, not even deducting our travel expenses?"

"Five hundred pounds…" Collins' Adams apple moved up and down. "Can't hardly say that figure without chokin'."

"Yes, just think of it…all that cash in our 'ands at one time. Five 'undred crisp one pound notes," Ned Ashworth said.

"Why does this bloke want to pay so much for an old, worn out corpse?" Collins sounded dubious.

"I don't know and I don't care. It's a chance for us to make a lot of money and get out from under. Frankly, this body is beginnin' to get me down. I'm tired of draggin' 'im all over the countryside. Time for somebody else to take charge and assume ownership."

"This Lord what's-his-name must have a scheme to make money off The Ripper."

Ned Ashworth took a deep breath and squinted back toward the tent in the meadow where they would open for business in ten minutes. A small group of ten or twelve people waited outside the roped-off area. "After doin' m'best negotiations with Lord Thurston, I've come to the conclusion that he wants this body to add to his collection. He has the money and doesn't care what it costs. He's like an art collector who has to have a one-of-a-kind original painting in his collection, damn the expense. Those rich blokes are all alike—they have to have the best, the rarest, the only. If there were three dozen Jack the Rippers around, Lord Thurston wouldn't care anything about buying ours."

"Just what kind of collection does he have, anyway?" Collins asked.

Ashworth glanced around the vacant field as if he might be overheard. "Just between you and me, it's very strange. He lives in that eight-hundred year old stone castle on the highest hill around. One of those old, gray places he inherited from ancestors away back. Has a reputation as a very odd duck. Never married, keeps to himself in that drafty old pile o'stones, takes part in some kind o'strange rituals, so the townsfolk say. Witches and demons—that sort o'thing. Now, it ain't my place to be passin' judgment on no man, mind you, but rumor has it he keeps a collection of skulls that once graced the gates of London town—Captain Kidd, Sir Thomas More, one or two of Henry the Eighth's wives what was beheaded, and who knows what other personages. And now he wants to add the actual, preserved, entire body, clothes and all—minus the brain o'course—of Jack the Ripper. Can't you just see it—him at a fancy masked ball with all his weird friends, standing around the alcohol tank, toasting Jack's health with goblets o'blood?"

"Ha! Ned, your imagination is runnin' amok."

"Well, my imagination has served us well all these years while we've managed to figure out ways to make the crowds pay to see us, to make them laugh and cry and gasp with astonishment and go away feelin' they got more than their shilling's worth."

"I'll give you credit, Ned. You have that. So be it, then. Where and when does Lord Thurston want to close the bargain?"

"He's waiting for us to send him word that we accept his offer. Then he'll be sending down a hearse drawn by six black horses and a mounted honor guard to collect Jack and escort him to his new home. Or, if the rumors are true, to his *old* home—Hell—in Thurston Castle."

"Amen."

EPILOGUE

The real Frederick George Abberline retired in 1892 after 29 years of service. Apparently, the strain of the unsolved Ripper case had no negative impact on his health as he lived to be 86 years old, dying in December, 1929.

Buffalo Bill Cody and his wife, Louisa, had a stormy relationship for years. She stayed at home when the show was on the road in the states or went overseas for months at a time. She was from a good family and enjoyed family life and a home. Cody enjoyed change and travel. She was very jealous of him, probably with good reason. A handsome, affable man who liked to drink and socialize, he attracted many good-looking younger women. There were rumors of infidelity. Lulu was given to throwing tantrums and broke up some costly hotel furniture in New York in 1898 when she thought he was entertaining another woman in his room. Unlike most modern marriages of movie stars, their marriage remained painfully intact until his death. In that era, divorce was not socially acceptable. A divorce could have hurt Cody's popularity and reputation. Yet, he finally did sue her for divorce in 1900, but the case was dismissed and Cody had to pay her court costs of $318. In spite of their public clashes they finally settled down in old age to put up with each other. Perhaps they even cared for each other. No one knows for sure.

Photographs of Louisa, or Lulu as he called her, taken about the time of their marriage show her to be reasonably pretty. Photos of her later in middle age reveal a homely, dowdy matron. Although

Bill Cody's hair grew white and began to thin, he always wore it long and carried himself with the air of a showman until his final days.

Cody's open, generous nature, along with inattention to business and money, caused him to be in debt much of his life. The slow passage of time, the changing tastes of the public, the fading of the frontier and a new generation becoming attracted to the movies eventually led to the end of Buffalo Bill's Wild West Show. But in the 1890s, it still played to packed arenas around the country. Two Pinkerton men traveled with the show in an effort to prevent pickpockets from working the crush of people who swarmed to get tickets. The frontier might have just passed into history, but millions of Americans wanted to see for themselves what it had been like. As the show rolled into the twentieth century, Cody's version of the wild west continued to draw thousands of spectators to every performance.

Still the ultimate showman, a white haired Cody, mounted on his magnificent horse, led the grand parade into the arena each day, bowed and waved his hat to his fans as always. He was giving thousands of Americans their last glimpse of what the real wild west had been like—Indians, settlers, the Custer massacre, holdups of the Deadwood stage, the hunting of the buffalo herds, the skillful cowboys and sharpshooters. But, after several announced farewell tours, the show finally faded away in 1916. Sick and in debt, he tried to continue performing, working for another man to whom he owed money. He finally died of prostate cancer in January, 1917 and is buried on a Colorado mountaintop.

In late October, 1901, a night train was rolling across North Carolina carrying most of the stock and personnel of Cody's Wild West Show to the season's last show dates in Virginia. At three in the morning, the locomotive plowed, head-on, into a freight train. Several stock cars in the forward part of the train were derailed and most of the horses killed. More fortunate were the humans who were in passenger coaches farther to the rear. Frank Butler was not injured and Annie Oakley was only bruised, although stories circulated that she'd been severely injured, and that her hair turned snow white within a few hours of the accident. It seems she was the one who fostered these stories. This turned out to be false, although by the following year her hair was fully white. There are conflicting stories as to the reason.

Frank and Annie decided it was time to leave the show, and they retired. But they didn't slow down. A year after leaving the show, she acted in a play written for her, titled, *The Western Girl.* Although she had no experience as an actress, the show toured for about a year to mostly favorable reviews.

But peaceful retirement was not to be. On August 11, 1903, a Hearst-owned Chicago newspaper broke the story that Annie Oakley had been caught stealing in order to get money to buy cocaine. According to the paper, Annie pled guilty and threw herself on the mercy of the court. The international star was destitute, dependent on drugs, and her striking beauty was gone, the reporter wrote. The erroneous story was picked up on the wire and spread all over the country.

Annie was furious. An imposter, pretending to be Annie Oakley, had ruined Annie's good reputation she'd spent all her life building up. Determined to clear her name, she filed twenty-five lawsuits for libel, demanding damages of $25,000 each against twenty-five newspapers. At her own expense, she traveled back and forth across the country, appearing in court when the cases came to trial. In all, she wound up suing fifty-five newspapers who'd printed the story without checking its validity. She either won judgments or settled out of court in nearly every case.

Stung by her actions, the wealthy and powerful William Randolph Hearst hired a detective to go to her hometown of Greenville, Ohio, to see if he could dig up any dirt on her—anything in her past that was detrimental to her reputation. He found nothing.

She spent six years traveling and testifying in court about her life, refuting the false story. And she won. It's not known if she actually profited from this relentless campaign to restore her reputation, but money was not the important thing. It's generally thought that she and Frank wound up losing money after they deducted all the travel expenses and lawyers' fees. But, in the end, she was vindicated, publicly exonerated and applauded by nearly everyone, including some of the newspapers, who apologized.

Annie and Frank were like rolling stones who couldn't settle down for long. They continued performing, now and then hooking up with a traveling show. For the remainder of their lives they hunted, vacationed in Florida in the winter, and she gave shooting lessons and clinics and exhibitions. Always willing to help the poor and less fortunate, she was active in charity work, giving many free exhibitions to raise money. About 1920, to the detriment of posterity, Annie had most of her gold medals melted down and the proceeds given to a tuberculosis sanitarium near Pinehurst, New Jersey.

During the patriotic fervor of the Great War, she discussed with former president, Theodore Roosevelt, the idea of raising a volunteer regiment of women who were skilled with arms and willing to use them, if necessary, to defend the home front. Roosevelt was adamantly against a regiment of women. She did visit many army camps in the states to inspire the soldiers by giving shooting exhibitions to young men who weren't even born when she was performing at the peak of her fame. They knew this petite, white haired lady only as a legend from the past.

While Annie was a staunch advocate of women carrying guns to protect themselves, she was not publicly in favor of women obtaining the right to vote. She continued to perform and even made $700 for a total of twenty-five minutes work at a shooting exhibition in 1922. She talked of making a comeback, but realized at age sixty-two it wasn't likely to happen. In November of that year she was riding in a car north of Daytona, Florida when the driver lost control and flipped over. Annie was pinned underneath with a fractured hip and right ankle. She spent several weeks in the hospital and for the rest of her life was required to wear a brace on her lower leg.

In failing health, she was visited by Will Rogers in 1926. He wrote a newspaper column about her. As a result of this column, Annie received a thousand letters from people all over the country.

Revered by the public to the end, Annie Oakley, a frail, white haired lady, passed away of pernicious anemia on November 3, 1926 at the age of 66. Her husband, Frank Butler, followed her in death only eighteen days later in Michigan. He was about 76. They are buried side by side in Darke County, Ohio.

As for Jack the Ripper…who knows? His end could have been just as I described it.

ABOUT THE AUTHOR

Tim Champlin was born John Michael Champlin in Fargo, North Dakota, the son of a school teacher, and a large animal veterinarian. He was reared in Nebraska, Missouri and Arizona where he was graduated from St. Mary's High School in Phoenix in 1955 before moving to Tennessee.

He received a Bachelor's degree from Middle Tennessee State College in Murfreesboro, and later earned an MA degree in English from Peabody College in Nashville, Tennessee (now part of Vanderbilt University).

After breaking into print in several national and regional magazines with short stories and non-fiction articles, he began his career as a novelist with *Summer of the Sioux* in 1981. To date, 30 of his historical novels have been published.

In *The Last Campaign*, he provides a compelling story of Geronimo's last days as a renegade leader. *Swift Thunder* is a thrilling story of the Pony Express. *Wayfaring Strangers* provides readers with an extraordinary tale of the California gold rush. All his stories contain unconventional plot twists, striking details and vivid, diverse characters. The wide-ranging narratives include lumber schooners sailing the West Coast, early-day wet-plate photography, tong wars in San Francisco's Chinatown, Basque sheepherders, the *Penitentes* of the Southwest, the stealing of Abraham Lincoln's body for ransom, a lost treasure of the Templars, and youthful time travel.

His last two novels, *Beecher Island* and *Tom Sawyer and the Ghosts of Summer*, were both published in 2010. He continues to write and publish short stories and articles.

He and his wife, Ellen, have three grown children and ten grandchildren. He retired from the U.S. Civil Service in 1994.

His hobbies include tennis, sailing, shooting, coin collecting, and typewriter collecting.

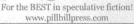
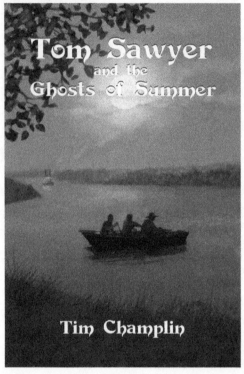

12-year-old Matt Lively is obsessed with trying to somehow stretch time to make summer last indefinitely. Convinced he is living the ideal time of life—in Missouri,1950, between the 7th and 8th grade—he longs to experience extraordinary adventures before he is forced to confront high school, and eventually, boring adulthood. Along with his best friends, Rob Linehart and Wally Carter, Matt begins the summer with pranks, problems and fun.

A mysterious and ominous tramp, Thatcher, accosts Matt and Rob and tells them things he should have no way of knowing. As Thatcher captures the boys' attention, he invites them back in time to save a life or two and recover a treasure, but mostly to change history in a way that will preserve *The Adventures of Tom Sawyer* and *Huckleberry Finn* for posterity.

Join Matt, Rob and Wally on their time-traveling adventure of self-discovery.

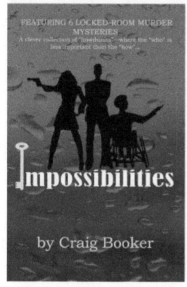

Impossibilities
by Craig Booker
ISBN-13: 978-1617060359

Welcome to the peculiar world of the Winters family!

Meet Cassandra Winter, a resourceful PI with a penchant for stumbling across murder mysteries which defy rational explanation. Along with her grandfather, J. Penderel Winter, a brilliant hypochondriac, and wisecracking Rufus Knight, a wheelchair-bound whizzkid with an IQ of 150, the three sleuths unravel impossible crimes, locked-room murders and bizarre mysteries.

Included in this collection: Sweet Miriam, The Regency Room, The Deveraux Staircase, Murder in Waiting, Grand Guignol and Spindleshanks.

Immerse yourself in the delightfully oddball universe of Impossibilities, where there is a solution to every perfect crime!

A Whodunit Halloween
Edited by Jessy Marie Roberts
ISBN-13: 978-0984261086

A spook-tastic collection of eleven mysteries that celebrate Halloween and the "whodunit" genre. Includes: Brain Food by Paul A. Freeman, Murder in the Corn Maze by Joan Bruce, The Canton House by Jessy Marie Roberts, Slightly Mummified by Diana Catt, A Bolt from the Blue by Craig Booker, Dad's Favorite Holiday by Rebecca J. Vickery, Resurrection Man by Tim Champlin, The Trick-or-Treat Killer by Mark Souza, The Murder of Charlie Dekker by Donna Dawson, Trapped Under Glass by Jessica A. Weiss & Cornfield Crucifixion by Gwen Mayo.